Song of the Mockingbird

My Journey with Josefina

by Emma Carlson Berne

★ American Girl®

17 18 19 20 21 22 23 QP 10 9 8 7 6 5 4 3 2 1

Special thanks to Sandra Jaramillo, former Director, Archives & Historical Services, New Mexico Records Center & Archives

This book is a work of fiction. Any similarity to real persons, living or dead, is coincidental and not intended by American Girl. References to real events, people, or places are used fictitiously. Other names, characters, places, and incidents are the products of imagination.

Cover image by Michael Dwornik and Juliana Kolesova
Piñón tree image by qingwa/iStock/Thinkstock

Cataloging-in-Publication Data available from the Library of Congress

For my dad—
with whom I've shared many adventures

Beforever™

The adventurous characters you'll meet in
the BeForever books will spark your curiosity
about the past, inspire you to find your voice
in the present, and excite you about your future.
You'll make friends with these girls as you share
their fun and their challenges. Like you, they are
bright and brave, imaginative and energetic,
creative and kind. Just as you are, they are
discovering what really matters: Helping others.
Being a true friend. Protecting the earth.
Standing up for what's right. Read their stories,
explore their worlds, join their adventures.
Your friendship with them will BeForever.

A Journey Begins

This book is about Josefina, but it's also about a girl like you who travels back in time to Josefina's world of 1824. You, the reader, get to decide what happens in the story. The choices you make will lead to different journeys and new discoveries.

When you reach a page in this book that asks you to make a decision, choose carefully. The decisions you make will lead to different endings. (Hint: Use a pencil to check off your choices. That way, you'll never read the same story twice.)

Want to try another ending? Go back to a choice point and find out what happens when you make different choices.

Before your journey ends, take a peek into the past, on page 184, to discover more about Josefina's time.

Josefina and her family speak Spanish, so you'll see some Spanish words in this book. You'll find the meanings and pronunciations of these words in the glossary on page 186. You'll find pronunciations of Spanish names on page 189.

Remember that in Spanish, "j" is pronounced like "h." That means Josefina's name is pronounced "ho-seh-FEE-nah."

The last bell chimes through the hallways, and I stack my notebooks and head for my locker. School is over for the day, and it has not been a success—again. Oh, on the surface things look fine. I'm talking to my teachers and smiling and playing kickball at recess. But underneath, here's the truth: I just don't want to be here. I want to be back at my old school—back in my old *life*.

I miss Chicago—the skyscrapers against the blue sky, traffic horns blaring, and cabs whizzing by on Michigan Avenue. The tall stone apartment buildings crowded together, the downtown lights sparkling on the lake. I miss rumbling above the streets on the screeching El on Saturday afternoons with Danielle to see shows. I miss my old school, with its huge gray stone front and twisty iron gates. I miss the halls crammed with kids, all talking and shouting to each other. I miss parties. I miss Drama Club—I was supposed to be the lead in *Annie.*

That was before my parents told me and my older brother, Henry, that we were moving. And where were we moving *to*?

The halls are almost empty now, and I wrench my

stuck locker door open. To Santa Fe, New Mexico, that's what they told us. I didn't even know where that was. I thought it was in actual Mexico.

We've been out here for two weeks now. It's so different here. Rocks, sand, cactus. Wind. Silence. And the buildings, a tan mud color, crouching low on the landscape under the sky that seems like a huge blue bowl turned upside down.

Our new house is made of mud too, like all of the houses out here—*adobe,* Dad calls it. He says that in the Southwest, houses have been built this way since ancient Indian times. The new house is out a ways from town, set alone on a little road. In our apartment in the city, I could look right into the windows of the family across the courtyard. They always looked so cozy in there, playing the piano or watching movies. Here, I look out at my new neighbors—big rocks. They *are* pretty—especially in the evenings when the sun turns them rosy red. But they sure aren't very cozy.

And at night, after the ruby-red sunset fades, there are no lights. No sounds either, except for this eerie noise that I thought at first was children screaming. Turns out it was only coyotes howling. I almost collapsed in relief when Dad told me.

Henry loves it out here, of course. He always likes anything new. And I'm *trying* to like it, too. After all, I've always loved adventures. But on our first day here, I went out with Daisy, my black German shepherd, for a walk. We took this winding little path that leads away from the house toward some kind of rocky hills. We were just wandering along, looking around, when we almost stepped on this strange little reptile right in our path. It looked like a cross between a toad and a lizard. Daisy barked at it and lunged toward it, and all of a sudden, it shot blood out of its *eyes* and splattered her right in the face. She yelped and I screamed and we both ran back toward the house as fast as we could. Mom said that thing is called a horny toad and it does that blood trick to ward off predators. After that, I managed to stop crying.

That was *not* the kind of adventure I had in mind. How will I ever feel at home in this place?

❀ *Turn to page 4.*

omeone's coming down the hall. It's Audrey again. She sits beside me in Mrs. McGlynn's class. I turn back to my locker quickly and bury myself in it, pretending to get out more books. I don't want to be mean, and actually I kind of like Audrey herself, but some little part of me keeps thinking that maybe if I'm miserable enough here, Mom and Dad will listen to me and let me move back to Chicago. I could live with Danielle!

"Hi," Audrey says. She's standing right beside me. I pull my head out of my locker.

"Oh! Hi," I say, as if I'm surprised to see her.

She smiles. "Want to walk over to La Plata Street? Some of my friends usually meet at the ice cream shop after school—you should come."

I know she's being really nice, but honestly, all I want to do is get home and Skype with Danielle. "No," I mumble. "I mean—no, I can't go today. I—um—have to catch the bus." Lame excuse.

Audrey's face falls slightly, but she shrugs. "Okay. Maybe tomorrow."

I just kind of nod, and Audrey trails along beside me down the echoing hallway. I slow to a stop at the

school bulletin board, and together we gaze at a flyer posted in the middle. *Love Acting?* it says. *Join the Skit Club! Auditions on Tuesday! A Part for Everyone!* I stare at it. I've always loved singing and dancing—my parents used to call me "Mockingbird," because I would sing every song I heard. Now they shorten it to "Birdy." But ever since leaving Chicago, I feel like I left the music in my heart behind too.

I can't help sighing, and Audrey glances at me. "Are you going to try out?" she asks.

I shake my head no. "Are you?"

She laughs. "Only if someone holds my hand. I get stage fright. Once when I was six, my mom had to come onstage during a piano recital and lead me off. I was frozen and couldn't move. I think I've been scarred for life."

I giggle in spite of myself. "That doesn't sound too bad. I once fell off the stage in the middle of a song. Right into the brass section." I realize we've walked all the way down the hall to the front doors.

Audrey pauses. "Sure you don't want to go for ice cream?"

I feel the laughter draining out of me and the

now-familiar heaviness setting in. "No thanks. I'd better get home." The late bus is waiting at the end of the circular driveway. It's my last chance unless I want to call Dad for a ride.

Audrey studies me for a minute as if she's trying to figure something out. Then she shrugs. "Whatever." She walks down the pink-brick path without looking back.

"Audrey, wait..." I call, but if she hears me, she doesn't turn around.

When she's disappeared, I start down the path and trudge slowly toward the idling yellow bus. I've hurt her feelings and I feel bad, but how can I expect her to understand? I just want to go home—all the way home.

✼

"Is that you, hon?" Dad calls out from the kitchen as I'm easing the side door closed. I wince. I was hoping to sneak upstairs and do what I've done every day since we arrived: chat with Danielle while I browse through our old pictures. No chance now.

Daisy bounds over to me, toenails skritching on

the tile. She joyfully paws me, her tongue lapping at my hands.

"Yeah!" I call back, trying to make my voice cheery. I sling my backpack into the hall closet and kiss Daisy's head. In the tiled kitchen, I find Dad standing at the counter, mixing some kind of thick yellow dough in a bowl. There's cornmeal on the floor, cornmeal in the sink, and cornmeal on his glasses.

"How was school?" Dad asks, scraping the dough from the wooden mixing spoon with his fingertips. "I don't think it's supposed to stick like that," he mutters to himself.

"What're you making?" I stick my head into the fridge to peruse the contents.

"*Masa.*" Dad starts laying out something that looks like damp leaves. I take a closer look. They *are* damp leaves. "Look, you spread this on these corn husks. Then you spoon in the filling—spiced shredded pork!"

I roll my eyes, though my face is still behind the fridge door. He and Mom have been seized with a passion for all things New Mexican since we've been out here. Yesterday they tried to give us scrambled eggs and green *chiles* wrapped in *tortillas* for breakfast.

"Remember Chicago hot dogs?" I ask Dad, digging a spoon into a jar of peanut butter. "Wouldn't you love one of those for dinner? With tomatoes and pickle relish and a poppy-seed bun?" My mouth waters just talking about it.

Dad nods and works two forks around in the pan of shredded pork. "Oh boy, I would. And next time we go back to visit, I'm eating one before we even get out of the airport. But meanwhile, how about homemade *tamales* for dinner?" He spoons pork into each of the corn husks and wraps them up like little packages.

I'm not too sure about food that comes wrapped up in leaves, like some kind of gourmet takeout for raccoons. "Sure." I can't muster much enthusiasm, and Dad smiles a little. I stick the spoon in the dishwasher and head for the stairs.

"Hey there." Dad's voice freezes me on the bottom step with one hand on the banister.

I peek back into the kitchen. "What?"

"Want to go for a walk?" He puts the *tamales* in a steamer basket waiting on the stove, then wipes his hands on a dishcloth and plucks his sunglasses from the hook by the door.

I open my mouth to respond and Dad holds up his hand. "Let me rephrase that. We're going for a walk. Daisy!" he calls.

Daisy capers around his feet, panting, and takes off the minute he opens the door.

Traitor, I tell her silently as we start off down the path toward the hills. *Don't you remember the horny toad?*

❋ *Turn to page 10.*

he late-afternoon sun is huge in the sky, which is so blue it almost hurts. The air is cool, but through it, I can feel the heat of the day coming off the rocks and sandy soil.

"Sage!" Dad says, pointing at a twiggy, silvery plant sprouting nearby. "And Indian paintbrush!" He bends to examine a small flower with a feathery, bright orange blossom. "Look at the orange color, honey."

"Yep." Dad *looooves* all of New Mexico's plants, animals, rock formations—you name it. "It's great."

Dad gives me a knowing look, but just nods. Daisy bounds ahead of us happily, barking at something only she can see. The deep green *piñón* trees line the base of the pinky-red rocks stacked against the horizon ahead of us. Suddenly, a mule deer bounds across the path right in front of us. I gasp and grab Dad's arm, and then, in a flash of white tail, it's gone, as if it never was.

"Wow!" I exclaim. "Did you see how fast it was?"

Dad grins at me. "Now there's something you wouldn't see on the Chicago streets."

I remember my bad mood and let my face lapse into a scowl again as we scuff our feet along the path.

"Birdy, Mom and I know how much you miss Chicago," Dad says quietly. "Bright lights, big city. Excitement. Adventure."

I steal a quick glance at him. He's picking his way around the rocks with his eyes on his boots.

"Yeah," I mumble.

"Believe it or not, we do too."

I can't help snorting in disbelief.

"We do." Dad raises his voice slightly for emphasis. "But we're trying to embrace our new home. We hope you will too. We hope you'll trust us that this will work out."

Don't count on it, I think, but I don't say anything. I just nod, which seems safest. We've reached the rocky hills at the end of the path. Daisy scrambles up on some bigger boulders and noses around the openings between them.

"That looks almost like a cave." I point out a larger opening, more to change the subject than anything else.

Dad climbs up on the rock beside Daisy and peers in. He looks around, his face excited. "It is! Here, come on. Let's peek in."

I grab his outstretched hand and haul myself up on

the rock too. We poke our heads and shoulders inside. It's cool and dark in there, and Dad clicks on the little pocket flashlight that always hangs from his key chain and holds it up. The ghostly white beam illuminates a rough rock floor and sloping walls that extend about ten feet back. Daisy slips inside and sniffs around the back of the cave.

"Want me to boost you in?" Dad offers. "It's stable— look up." He shines the flashlight up at the roof and we both laugh. It's more than stable—it's solid rock.

"Sure," I say, a little excitement bubbling up. I squeeze in and peer out at Dad from the opening. I can just stand up. Looking from the inside out makes me feel like I've entered a separate world—a little cold, dark, alien space. Outside, the high desert spreads big, hot, and blue-green-yellow. It seems miles away.

"See anything interesting?" Dad asks. He passes his flashlight in, and I scan the walls with it.

"Just rock—" I start to say, and then I see Daisy nosing under a pile of stones by the rear wall, digging with her front feet. She sticks her nose into the pile, sniffing deeply. She backs up and barks once, a sharp, excited bark.

"Daisy's found something in there," I say.

"Careful," Dad warns. "It might be a snake."

Moving slowly, I bend over and shine the flashlight into the little scattered pile of stones. There's no snake, but one of the rocks is shaped oddly. I move closer. It's not a rock at all, I realize. It's an object made of clay.

"Dad—it's some kind of..." I bend closer. It's a bird-shaped figure, made of gray clay and coated with dust.

I pick it up. It's about the size of my hand, and hollow. Traces of yellow paint glow in the dimness. As I turn it, I see there's a hole at the end of the bird's tail and another at its mouth, and a few small holes along its back. "It's a whistle. Or maybe a little flute." The clay is strangely warm and smooth.

I clutch the figure tightly and follow Daisy out through the opening.

✻ *Turn to page 14.*

n the sunlight, Dad and I examine the flute. He points out lines scored in the clay to represent the bird's wings and tail feathers. "This little flute is probably from the early nineteenth century."

Dad pushes his sunglasses up on his forehead and peers at the flute more closely. "Handmade, most likely for casual use." Dad is a professor of Southwestern art at the university, so he knows about stuff like this. "It's in great shape. It was probably hidden in those rocks for a long time—that's why it hasn't fallen apart from time and moisture." He claps me on the shoulder. "What an adventure! Let's go find Mom—she'll want to see our new treasure too."

We start back to the house, me cradling the bird flute in my hands and Daisy trotting beside us. But when we reach the yard, I slow down. Through the big picture windows, I can see Mom and Henry in the kitchen. They must have just gotten home. She picks up Henry at the high school on her way home from the health center—she's a social worker there.

I don't want to face the bustle inside, Mom asking questions, Henry raving *again* about how cool it is here and how he's going rock climbing or spelunking with

José or Dave or Simone or some other awesome friend he seems to have made instantly.

"Actually, I think I'm going to just chill out here for a while," I tell Dad. I hoist myself up on one of the bigger boulders that sits about ten yards from the back of the house. From here, I can see right into the house—but I'm still alone. "I need to relax."

He smiles and nods. "Okay. We'll show Mom and Henry the flute at dinner." He pauses for a moment with one hand on the door. "Why don't you keep that flute safe with you, Birdy? At least until we figure out if a museum should have it. For now, though—it's a little gift from Santa Fe to you." He disappears through the side door.

❋ *Turn to page 16.*

Once Dad's gone, I draw my knees up to my chin and loop my arms around them. Daisy lies down beside me, licking at her side and flopping her tail. The rock underneath us is warm, like a heater, which feels good in the cool air. The first afternoon we were here, I was shocked when the temperature plunged twenty degrees as soon as the sun dipped behind the hills. Now I know that the high desert can be as chilly at night as it is hot during the day.

I rub the flute idly between my fingers and gaze out at the hills. Some have flattened tops; some are rounded. The dark dots of the pines stud their sides, like cloves stuck in an orange. Just in front of me, three hills, taller and thinner than the others, rise like rounded spires into the sky. *Almost like the Chicago skyline,* I think to myself. If I squint my eyes, I can practically see the tower of the John Hancock Center. The sun flashes between the spires for a moment, blinding me. I look down at the flute in my hand and turn it over.

I can see the faint indentations where the maker pressed his or her fingers while molding it. The delicate head of the bird flows into the rounded body, and the tail balances gracefully behind it. There is a

tiny chip out of the very end of the tail.

Carefully, I raise the flute to my lips and blow. The delicate note drifts away on the breeze. I place my fingers over the holes and try a scale. The notes are clear and light. I stumble through "When the Saints Go Marching In," and Daisy raises her head and looks at me with her soulful dog eyes.

I lower the flute. "Do you like that, girl? Me too." And I do like it. I like it almost more than anything else I've heard since we moved.

My fingers brush a bit of roughness on the bottom of the flute, and I turn it over. There, carved in letters so small I didn't notice them before, is a word. I squint at it. *María.* This was María's flute, then. The maker must have carved her name in it when it was made so long ago. I trace the curves of the name with the tip of one finger. I can still feel the tiny ridges where the sharp point scored the wet clay. It's like reaching through time.

I lift the flute to my lips again, but before I can blow, the notes of a bird's song float over to me. I lower the flute. A mockingbird is sitting on the branch of a pine shrub only a few feet away. It sings again.

Trill-trillEE. Trill-trillEE. Its smooth gray chest swells with the song, and its bright black eye gleams.

I look down at the flute, and my heart gives a little jump. It's a mockingbird! The flute is modeled after a mockingbird—same plump breast, same long, balancing tail. The bird sings again. *Trill-trillEE. Trill-trillEE.*

I smile to myself. My parents didn't call *me* Mockingbird for nothing. I raise the flute to my lips and form the notes with my tongue and fingers: *Trill-trillEE. Trill-trillEE.* The mockingbird's song flows from my mockingbird flute.

But as soon as the notes are out, I feel myself topple suddenly, pitching forward, falling, clutching at nothing, aware only of the flute still squeezed in my hand. Darkness slams down over me like an iron door.

❄

I open my eyes. My cheek is lying in dirt, and my whole body aches. I push myself up onto my hands and look around.

I'm sprawled at the bottom of the boulder—I must have fallen and gotten knocked out. Daisy's gone. My temples are throbbing, and my hands are covered with

dust and dirt. The bird flute is lying a few feet away. I push myself up a little more and reach for it. But something about the day seems different now, and for a moment I can't figure it out. Then I know—it's the light. The sun seems to have gotten higher. My heart gives a quick thump. *Higher?* That's weird.

I sit up and shake my head, and then I squint at the sun again. It *is* higher, and hotter. I'm sweating in my white blouse.

Wait. *My white blouse?* I was wearing a T-shirt! I look down at myself and freeze. I'm wearing different clothes. A puffy blouse, and a long flouncy skirt with a fringed sash around my waist. And moccasins. Moccasins! They look strangely like my bedroom slippers, and for a brief, insane moment I wonder if my mother came out here and dressed me in these clothes while I was knocked out. I should go ask her.

I turn toward the house, and my heart freezes in my chest like a galloping horse at the edge of a cliff.

The house is gone.

❋ *Turn to page 27.*

I open my eyes.

I'm outside. I'm lying on a big rock—the boulder outside my house. Daisy! Daisy is beside me. She's still licking her side. I'm wearing jeans again! A T-shirt! I sit up and twist around so fast, I almost fall off the rock. There's my house! I can see Mom and Henry inside, talking to Dad.

I look down at my hand. The whistle is clutched in it. My mouth is suddenly very dry. "Daisy," I whisper. She looks up at me and thumps her tail. "Something very strange is happening." She licks my hand and then rests her chin on her paws.

I prop my elbows on my knees and cover my eyes with my hands. *Okay. Think.* Aside from the fact that this is the freakiest thing that has ever happened to me in—oh, my entire life—these seem to be the facts: First, somehow, I am traveling back and forth through time. Second, playing the mockingbird song will send me into the past and then bring me back to my own time. Third, for whatever reason, maybe decided by the Time-Traveling Council of the Universe or something, no time in the present passes while I'm in the past. Go figure.

I stare down at the flute. The dot marking the bird's eye looks back at me. I could go back. *Why not? I seem to hear the bird say. Didn't that girl Josefina seem nice?*

Why not? I respond silently. Why not? Because it was scary, that's why! Cool, but scary. On the other hand, I *have* been looking for a little adventure, haven't I?

I take another look back at the house. Henry has taken a paper from his backpack and is showing it to Mom and Dad. I never thought our flat *adobe* house could look so much like home. Part of me longs to run inside to my family. But on the other hand . . . they'll never know I'm gone.

❋ *To stay in the present,*
   turn to page 45.

❋ *To go back to Josefina's time,*
   turn to page 47.   ✓

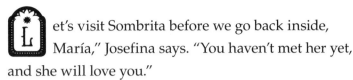et's visit Sombrita before we go back inside, María," Josefina says. "You haven't met her yet, and she will love you."

Sombrita must be another sister. Josefina didn't mention her before. Or perhaps she's a servant. "Sure," I agree.

Josefina leads me around the side of the house. "There's Sombrita," Josefina says. "Isn't she lovely?" She points under a tree near the house.

"Where?" I can't see anything but the goats that sniffed me when I first arrived.

"Right there." Josefina is pointing to one of the animals. "She's the little gray-and-white one."

"Sombrita is a goat?" I ask and burst out laughing.

"Well, yes!" Josefina looks a little confused. "I've had her since she was just a baby."

"I thought she was another sister!"

Josefina chortles. "Poor sister—with horns and yellow eyes!" Then we're both laughing so hard, we have to clutch each other to keep from falling over. I realize I'm having more fun than I've had since leaving Chicago. Being with Josefina is almost like being with Danielle.

The little goat bounces up to us like she's on springs. She sniffs my legs and nudges me with her hard head. I give her a tentative pat. Her fur is very soft, like a puppy's, and when I scratch her, I can feel the tiny buds of horns at the top of her head.

"Oh, Sombrita." I dissolve into giggles again. "We don't mean to make fun of you. Your yellow eyes are perfect for you." The goat gazes up at me as if she understands what I'm saying. Daisy would probably like her. They'd be friends, just like Josefina and me. "Where did you get her, Josefina?"

"Oh, it was special," my friend says. She kneels on the ground, and the little goat climbs into her lap like a dog. She reaches up and sniffs Josefina's face. "Her mother, Florecita, died right after Sombrita was born. Papá thought the baby wouldn't live, but I begged him to let me keep her." Sombrita stretches her front legs up on Josefina's shoulder.

"I fed her carefully, and she grew stronger and stronger." The little goat nimbly leaps right up on Josefina's shoulder, as if she's a ladder, and I squeal.

Josefina laughs and reaches up behind her to pull Sombrita back down off her shoulders. She holds the

little goat up to her cheek and nuzzles her soft fur. "I promised I'd always take care of her. Now I can't imagine not having her as my friend."

I drop down on my knees next to Josefina and stroke Sombrita's back. She squirms around, and her little tongue laps out as if tasting my cheek.

Josefina hugs her tighter and then carefully sets her on her feet. "There, little one. Run and play." Sombrita obeys as if she can understand the words. With her little tail wagging constantly and her ears flopping, she rears up on her hind legs, then drops down and scampers over to a log lying under the tree. She jumps up on it as if she's on a trampoline and then runs up and down the length.

"Woo-hoo, Sombrita!" I shout, applauding.

Josefina looks over at me as if she's never heard anyone say that before—which, I realize, she probably never has—and echoes me. "Woo-hoo, Sombrita!" she calls.

We stand up slowly, dusting off our skirts, and just then, a bell bongs somewhere far away. I must look startled because Josefina says gently, "Do you remember how the church bells call us to prayer?" She bows

her head, and it takes me a minute to realize that she's praying. She must be pretty religious.

Josefina opens her eyes as a sweaty man on a horse rides up and halts in front of us. I almost jump out of my skin.

"Miguel, you're back," she says, and Tía Dolores appears in the doorway, wiping her hands on her apron.

"There are no signs of enemies in our hills," Miguel says, leaning over the saddle pommel. "This *cautiva* must have wandered far from the place where she escaped."

Tía Dolores's face relaxes. "Ah. Good."

"Thank heaven," Josefina says. Then she turns businesslike. "Now, I'll help you remember how to do things. We'll work together, so you can learn again. Would you like to go collecting with me in the hills?" she asks. "If Tía Dolores says we may, of course." She looks over at her aunt, who nods. "Teresita has asked me to gather plants for dyes. Or we can gather squashes from the garden instead, if you are not feeling strong enough for an expedition. Then I'll show you how to string slices of squash to dry for the winter."

The hills still sound a little scary. What if enemies showed up while we were out there? I shiver as I think of being swept up onto an enemy's horse. But I know Miguel has just made sure we're safe, and it would be fun to hike with Josefina out in the wind and sunshine—more fun than with Dad, probably. Josefina seems like someone who's not afraid of adventures.

❋ *To collect squashes from the garden, turn to page 31.* ↵

❋ *To go on an expedition in the hills, turn to page 36.* ↵

Another kind of house is there instead. It's *adobe* too, but much, much bigger than ours, with only a few teeny windows and a giant wooden front door. It looks like a fortress. The driveway is gone too, and the cars, and the telephone lines. Instead, a few chickens are pecking near the door, and—I squint—are those *goats*? They can't be. Probably the neighbor's dogs have escaped again. I rub my eyes. No. They are goats.

Panic wells up in me, and I have a feeling like I'm drowning. Is this what it feels like to go crazy? Then instantly, the explanation occurs to me, and it's so simple, I almost laugh. I'm dreaming. That's the answer, of course. Why didn't I think of it before?

Just then, a girl comes out of a little door cut right into the big front door of the house-that-is-not-mine. She's about my age, ten, with a long, shiny, dark brown braid, and she's carrying a big empty basket. She stops when she sees me, and we stare at each other. Then she drops the basket and rushes over to me.

"Oh my goodness, are you lost?" She looks me up and down. "You're covered in dirt. Are you hurt?"

Whoa, I'm kind of freaking out again. The words coming out of her mouth aren't English—but I can

understand her. Then I remind myself: *I'm dreaming.*
Weirdness is normal. The sound of the girl's words is
familiar too—Spanish! Just like in Spanish class back
home. I don't know much, though—I only studied it for
one year. I wonder if this girl knows English.

"I think I do need help," I say, but then I snap
my mouth shut. I can feel my eyes bulging. That was
Spanish that came out of my mouth. Very carefully,
I try again. "I was just sitting on this rock—" Still
Spanish. But I can understand what I'm saying! And
the girl is nodding, like she can understand me too.

All right. Apparently, it's an all-Spanish-speaking
dream. That's cool. I can go with it.

The girl is peppering me with questions, but I can't
stop staring at her clothes. She's dressed just like me—
long blouse, full, gathered skirt, a long sash, and moccasins. She has a little leather pouch tied to the sash at
her waist. And the house and the chickens... This must
be a dream taking place in old-fashioned days. But it's
weirdly vivid. The most real dream I've ever had.

"I'm Josefina Montoya," the girl tells me. "What's
your name? Where on earth did you come from? How
did you arrive at our *rancho*?"

I look around. She must mean this place. It *is* like a ranch: Off in the distance, beyond a row of golden cottonwood trees, fields are spread out like blankets, and men in wide hats are working in them. As I watch, two men ride toward them on horses. A big herd of sheep is milling around bleating in a kind of enclosure made of sticks. But Josefina is still staring at me expectantly.

"Um, is that where I am—your *rancho*?" I ask. The Spanish words are starting to feel more natural.

Josefina's big dark eyes look concerned. She reaches out and fingers a long tear in my skirt, then touches my forehead. "You have a big streak of dirt here. Have you hit your head?" Her voice is gentle. "Here, let's go inside. Tía Dolores will help you."

Josefina leads me toward the huge wooden door. We pass the goats, which sniff me interestedly. The little door cut into the big door stands open. I catch my foot on the high threshold and stumble, but Josefina quickly catches my arm. "You're not well," she says.

I nod. That is certainly true. I *must* not be well, because whatever is happening feels more and more like reality and less and less like a dream. Perhaps I have sunstroke? Dust-stroke?

Josefina squeezes my hand. Her fingers are strong, and I feel comforted. "I'll make you chamomile tea. Tía Magdalena says that's the best for calming nerves."

I have no idea who Tía Magdalena is, but I'm going to do whatever Josefina says. I'm thirsty, dirty, and confused. I think of the chamomile tea that Mom always makes me when I'm sick. Tears well up unexpectedly at the thought, and I swipe my hand fast across my eyes.

"Oh dear!" Josefina clasps both of my hands tightly. "Don't worry. You're safe now, whatever's happened to you. We're going to take care of you."

I nod, not trusting my new Spanish-speaking voice, which I'm sure would be clogged with tears.

Just as Josefina leads me through the doorway, something makes me turn to the horizon. There, like Chicago's skyscrapers, are the three rounded spires, standing tall against the blue New Mexico sky.

❋ *Turn to page 39.*

I 'd like to see your garden," I say.

Josefina smiles. "Of course. But first you'll need a *rebozo* to shade your face from the sun. You must have lost yours on the journey."

My what?

Josefina runs off through one of the doorways and is back in a moment with a large piece of cloth that I realize is a shawl. "Here you go." She has one too, I notice. It's been hanging around her shoulders, but now she pulls it up over her head. I copy her, which is hard since the slippery wool keeps sliding around on my hair. Then Josefina plucks two big empty baskets from the corner of the entryway. She hands one to me. "Come with me. The garden is behind the house."

I almost drop the big basket as I try to balance it on my hip as gracefully as Josefina. I might be an expert at traveling back and forth in time, but I can see I'm going to have a lot to learn in Josefina's world.

I follow Josefina out through the courtyard at the back of the house. We nod and smile at a servant carrying a huge earthen jug of water on her head. She steadies it with one hand, and there's a ring of cloth between her head and the bottom of the jug—that

must help her balance it. It looks like a lot of work
just for one jug of water. I picture the kitchen faucet at
home—endless water, all the time. I bet Josefina's family would like that.

The doors in the walls are closed, but in one corner,
a mass of flowers blazes like a rainbow fallen to earth.
Josefina pushes open a small rear door and leads me to
a high fence made of sticks. Sombrita bounces over to us
and tumbles around our ankles as Josefina unlatches a
gate to reveal a big garden. It reminds me of one of the
blankets from the house—stripes of red, green, and
yellow, with splashes of orange. "No, Sombrita, you
know you're not allowed in! These vegetables are for
eating this winter, not snacking on now," Josefina tells
the goat, and pushes her gently away from the gate
before she closes it behind us.

She walks carefully down a row of plants, and
I follow. She kneels down beside the bushy green vines
heavy with yellow squashes, and from the bottom of
her basket produces two small, sharp knives. She hands
one to me and begins busily cutting yellow squashes
from their prickly, sprawling vines. I kneel beside her
and clumsily follow her example. The late-afternoon

sun is hot on our backs, and all around us is the rich, dank odor of the vegetables and the earth.

There are no sounds except the whisper of the wind, and far away, the cry of a hawk. I've never been in a place so quiet—even in our new house, you can still hear the hum of traffic from the highway or a phone ringing. "Do you have any neighbors?" I ask, trying not to slice my own thumb off as I struggle with the big woody squash stems.

"No, not near the *rancho*," Josefina answers cheerfully. "The nearest neighbors are in the village. It's not far. Only a half-hour walk," she tells me, expertly slicing through a small stem. "And Santa Fe, where Abuelito and Abuelita live, is only half a day's ride by wagon."

Wagons. This is sounding like Laura Ingalls Wilder.

"So you're all alone out here?" I say. "Isn't that scary?"

Josefina laughs as if I've made a clever joke. "I'm far from alone! There are my sisters, of course, and Papá, and Tía Dolores—she's my mamá's sister and came to live with us last year. And Ana's husband Tomás and their two little boys. And Teresita, and Carmen the cook, and her husband Miguel, and all

the other servants and farmhands who live here."

"That *is* a lot of people," I agree, finally cutting through the tough squash stem and placing the vegetable in my basket. I shuffle forward on my knees and reach for another one. "And there's your mother too, right? I haven't seen her yet."

Josefina's hands stop moving, and her head bows.

"I'm sorry. What is it?" I reach over and put my hand on her back.

She looks up, and I see that her beautiful dark eyes are brimming with tears. "Mamá died almost two years ago." She swallows hard and takes a deep breath. "Tía Dolores has been staying here, to help care for us, and she has been a great comfort. But I miss Mamá still."

I feel my own eyes getting wet. "I'm sorry, Josefina." She nods, and we are both still, thinking our separate thoughts.

"You know what it is to miss something," Josefina says. "You had to leave your whole family and your home."

I know that Josefina is imaging a *cautiva*'s life, but her words still ring true for me. Our brownstone apartment building and the view down our old Chicago street suddenly float up in front of me, and my stomach twists with sadness. I almost gasp. "I do know what it is to miss something," I whisper. I mean for only the squashes to hear, but a tanned hand suddenly reaches over and covers mine. I look up into Josefina's face. Her eyes are still wet, but she is smiling.

"Destiny has brought us together as friends, María," she says. "We have lost precious things, but we have found each other."

Her words feel very true, and suddenly I feel happy again. "Yes," I say. "I've needed a friend."

"And here, you have one!" she tells me.

❀ *Turn to page 55.*

'm up for an expedition," I say, trying to be brave.

I follow Josefina back into the house through the now-deserted courtyard, washed with sun, and into another room. We step into the dim space, and I pause to let my eyes adjust. The doorway is a hot, bright rectangle, but in here, everything is cool and shadowy. It's like the cave where I found the flute, but it holds different treasures. A huge wooden structure I recognize as a loom takes up most of the room. White strands of yarn are taut across its top, fanning out as if spun by a tidy spider. Some blue strands are woven halfway across the web of white yarn. Big hanks of bright wool hang from pegs on the walls—yellow, blue, gray, black. My eyes are drawn to a red that glows like fire against the soft tan *adobe*. Against another wall, baskets of fluffy raw wool are lined up.

A whole room, just for weaving.

A soft rustle draws my eye to the corner. Teresita is kneeling there at what I guess is a loom hung on the wall. Two heavy beams are suspended horizontally a few inches from the ceiling. Another beam hangs near the floor, also horizontally. And a third, smaller beam

is suspended about halfway down. More white yarn is strung tightly on the beams from the top to the bottom. I watch Teresita pass a small ball of gray yarn through the white strands and push it down on top of other strands of gray she's already woven. The blanket she's working on has a zigzag pattern in black and red.

Teresita looks over at us, but her hands never stop moving the gray yarn back and forth. "Are you ready to find rabbit brush?" she asks.

"*Sí,*" Josefina says. "Rabbit-brush flowers make this yellow color, María." She gestures toward a blanket folded on a table in the corner. Sunny stripes alternate with black.

"There should be plenty in the hills," Teresita says.

"And we'll find it," Josefina assures her.

A short while later, I find myself striding from the house with a basket over my arm, just like Josefina. My flute is tucked into a leather pouch at my waist just like Josefina's. Josefina pulls the shawl that's been draped around her shoulders over her head in one fluid movement. She glances at me. The shawl she's just given me is still around my shoulders. The sisters wore theirs the same way in the house. "Don't you

need to pull up your *rebozo*?" Josefina asks, with a hint of surprise in her voice.

"I'm good," I say, but then I catch the surprise on my friend's face. Oops. Wrong answer. I pull the silky wool shawl up onto my head. Another rule for girls, apparently. There seem to be a lot of them.

Sombrita has decided to accompany us and bounds ahead on her springlike legs. Behind us, Miguel is following with another basket over his arm.

"Josefina," I whisper, hurrying to keep up. "Does Miguel need some rabbit brush too?"

Josefina giggles. "No, he's going with us as our chaperone and guardian, of course."

I turn this over as we climb into the rising hills behind the house. I guess Josefina and her sisters don't go out without someone watching over them. That makes sense, though—after all, I was supposed to have been captured. And maybe that's why Josefina's house reminds me of a fortress.

I shiver. How dangerous *is* this world?

❀ *Turn to page 58.*

I follow Josefina into a large open courtyard with a floor of hard dirt and smooth stones. Walls surround the courtyard on all sides. I glimpse a walkway leading to another courtyard at the back of the house. The courtyard walls have many door openings, and I catch glimpses of rooms beyond. There is a round clay thing like a kiln in one corner of this courtyard, some more chickens pecking randomly about, and baskets of shiny red peppers sitting around.

Josefina leads me over to three girls and a woman sitting together in the middle of the courtyard. They're dressed just like her, but the older two girls and the woman wear their hair in low buns. The younger girl has a braid, like Josefina and me. "My aunt is staying here at the *rancho* with my sisters and me for a while, to help us," she tells me on the way.

"Tía Dolores," Josefina says to the woman, "I've found this girl wandering outside. She's lost, I think. May she rest here at our home?"

Josefina's voice sounds different—lower, respectful. The other girls stop what they're doing and stare at me, open-mouthed. I try not to stare too much back.

Tía Dolores jumps to her feet. She looks at my face,

touches my brow. "Where in heaven did you come from?" she murmurs. Then she stops herself. "But you must be tired. Questions can wait. Josefina is right— you must rest here."

Josefina introduces me. "This is Ana, my oldest sister. She's married and has two little boys. And these are my other sisters, Francisca and Clara." The girls all have piles of the red peppers in their laps. Josefina hasn't mentioned her mother—maybe she's somewhere in the house.

Ana smiles at me kindly. "Sit here by me. Josefina, I think our visitor might like a cool cloth for her face." I sink down next to Ana and squirm a little on the woolen blankets spread on the hard ground. The sisters look as comfortable as if they were sitting in armchairs.

"May I make our visitor some chamomile tea also?" Josefina asks Tía Dolores.

"Yes, please do," the aunt says. She has clear, understanding gray eyes, and her hair is a deep, deep auburn red.

Josefina disappears through one of the doorways that open onto the courtyard. I sit still beside Ana. This is all feeling very real. Very, very real, I have to say.

I claw my fingernails into my palm so hard, it hurts. Pain. Don't they say you can't feel pain in dreams?

Josefina appears with a steaming cup, which I almost grab at to distract my spinning mind. Josefina wipes my face with a cool, damp cloth, which feels wonderful against my dusty skin. I take a tentative sip of the tea, which is in a kind of pottery mug, like the ones Mom buys at art fairs.

The warmth spreads through me and I feel my muscles unclenching. I let out a deep breath and smile at the sisters, who are watching me anxiously. They smile back and return to sorting the red peppers piled in their laps, but I can sense that they're dying to ask me more questions.

"What's that in your hand?" Clara asks. Everyone looks, and I realize I'm still clutching the clay bird flute.

"It's my flute," I say, but even as the words leave my mouth, I realize that the flute looks different now— newer, not as dusty. The chip off the bird's tail is gone too. I swallow. The strange thoughts are pushing in further.

"May I see the flute?" Francisca asks.

I hand it to her, and she runs her fingers over the

markings, like Dad did. "This is beautifully made," she says. "It's so graceful." She turns the flute over. "María. Is that your name?"

They all look at me. I nod uncertainly. I don't know what else to do.

I'm having the increasingly certain feeling that this is not a dream—but if it's not, then what *is* happening? I have to get myself alone, to think for a minute.

"I—I'm feeling a bit dizzy," I say to Tía Dolores. "Is there a place I could lie down?"

"Did you hit your head outside?" Her brow creases in concern. "You must rest," she says. "Josefina, take María to your sleeping *sala.*"

Who's María? Oh, right. That's me.

"Here, come this way." Josefina leads me through one of the doorways into a small room with plain *adobe* walls. Big rolls of soft material are stacked against one wall. A blue-and-white blanket hangs from a rod on the other wall. I lean in to examine it and draw in my breath.

"Josefina, this is beautiful!" I say. The fibers are woven so smoothly together, I can hardly see them. The blue stripes are the deep blue color of the Santa Fe sky.

Josefina looks down at her feet and smiles shyly. "Thank you. It's the first blanket I wove by myself."

"You *wove* this?" I look more closely. "Wow!" Mom just recently taught me to sew on a button. Weaving a whole blanket would be like me cooking Thanksgiving dinner for twenty. "I wish I could do that."

"You'll be comfortable here," Josefina says. At first, I don't know how that's possible, since there's no bed in sight, and then I realize that she is unrolling one of the big bundles. It's bedding—a sheepskin and some more of the amazing blankets. "Is this your bed?" I try not to sound too incredulous. I don't want to insult her or anything. They sleep on the floor?

Josefina gives me a strange look. "Of course. Clara's is there, and Francisca's is there. Ana and Tomás— that's Ana's husband—have their own room."

So not only does she sleep on the floor, she also shares with both her sisters. I flash on my own four-poster bed at home—in my own room.

Josefina helps me lie down and covers me with a woven blanket that has a pattern like diamonds. The sheepskins are surprisingly comfortable and smell vaguely like my favorite wool sweater. "Here, close your eyes," Josefina says, and I do.

But the moment she's gone, I sit up and try to think. This is not a dream. It's—something else. A mystery. How did I get here? The flute. The flute came here— wherever I am—with me. I was sitting on the rocks outside the house, and I played it, like this. I blow a tentative note. Actually, it wasn't exactly like that. I was listening to the mockingbird and then I played its song. I moisten my lips and place my fingers on the holes. *Trill-trillEE. Trill-trillEE.*

Then it happens again. I feel myself falling through space. Everything is dark. I try to breathe and can't, and then—*wham!*

❋ *Turn to page 20.*

ome is right in front of me, I think. *It's where my family is.* But maybe I had to lose them—temporarily—before I could realize how much they mean to me.

With my heart feeling lighter than it has in a long time, I climb off the rock, and Daisy bounds down after me. The afternoon sun touches the *adobe* of the house with a warm, golden light. I never thought this funny flat-roofed house could look so welcoming. But maybe that's because I didn't realize that it's actually what the house *contains* that matters.

I pull open the side door, and Daisy pushes in ahead of me. My family's faces turn toward me—familiar, smiling. "There you are, honey," Mom says. She comes over and gives me a little hug. "I want to hear about your day."

"Hey, sis," Henry says. "Looked for you after school—I thought you might want a ride. I guess we missed each other."

I lean against the counter, considering my brother's words. Dad moves over to the stove and checks the *tamales.* They smell delicious. "You know, Henry," I tell him, "I think you might be right. We *have* missed

each other. Except that now I'm home. For good."

I smile at him and he smiles back, looking slightly confused. I reach into the cupboard by the sink and grab a stack of plates. The *tamales* are ready. And I'm starving.

❀ *The End* ❀

To read this story another way and see how different choices lead to a different ending, turn back to page 21.

ee you soon, Daisy-girl," I whisper. I raise the flute to my lips. *Trill-trillEE. Trill-trillEE.*

And just like that, I'm back in the plain little room. The diamond-patterned blanket is spread over me. I'm wearing the blouse and the skirt and—I peek under the blanket—the moccasins. My mind feels much clearer now that I know I'm not going crazy, and I throw back the blanket with new energy. I climb off the sheep-skin and clumsily roll it up against the wall again. It's heavier than it looks.

"María!" From the courtyard, Josefina spots me peering out of the doorway. She motions me over. "Come sit with us." The sisters have sorted the peppers, it seems, and two big baskets of perfect, shiny ones sit nearby. Josefina, Tía Dolores, and Clara are now sitting around a big pile of roasted ears of corn, pulling back the pale gold husks and removing the dark silk.

Josefina pats the ground beside her and I sink down, trying to tuck my bulky skirt underneath me like the others. They're watching me, which makes my cheeks hot. I grab an ear of corn and awkwardly wrestle with the leaves.

"Where is your family, María?" Tía Dolores asks.

Her hands move without stopping, smoothly stripping back the husk and revealing rows of yellow kernels. "We must return you to them—they must be very worried."

"I, um..." I look down at the half-husked ear in my lap. "I'm not sure exactly where they are." How could I even begin to explain?

"Do you mean you've gotten lost?" Clara asks, her eyebrows knitting together with concern.

"Something like that." *Lost in time,* I think—but how can I tell them I'm from the *future*? "I've had a really... strange experience that brought me here."

Everyone is quiet for a moment, and then from behind me, someone says, "We *cautivas* sometimes find it hard to talk about our experiences."

I turn around. In a corner of the courtyard sits an older woman I hadn't noticed before. Her face is deeply wrinkled and tanned. She wears her hair in a different style from Tía Dolores—a twist bound by colorful threads. She is rubbing a pot with something—sand, it looks like. She must be scrubbing it—Mom cleans pots like that when we're camping.

"Oh, a *cautiva*!" Josefina draws in her breath, and

her hand creeps over mine and squeezes my fingers.

Francisca and Clara murmur and shake their heads, looking distressed.

That word they keep saying—*captive.* They think I've been taken captive? Like kidnapped?

"My poor child!" Tía Dolores says, and I feel her draw my head briefly to her shoulder in a kind of hug.

"María, this is Teresita, our servant," Tía Dolores says. She pauses, as if unsure of something, and then looks at Teresita, who nods as if giving permission. "She was also a *cautiva.*"

Teresita's hand goes around and around in the pot. "I too was taken from my people, the Navajos, by enemies when I was a little girl. Just as enemies took you from your people, the Spanish."

Huh? Captive? Enemies of my people? The others must know what Teresita is talking about, though, because they are nodding sympathetically. It sounds like Teresita was sort of kidnapped when she was younger, and now everyone thinks that the same thing happened to me.

"How old were you when you were captured?" Francisca asks.

"I—" *How old was I?*

"Did the Indians treat you kindly?" Clara interrupts.

"I, um..." I stutter. *Indians?*

"Did you escape?" Josefina asks. "You must have wandered a long time, you were so dusty when I found you. Who gave you the Spanish clothes?"

The questions are coming fast, and I'm getting flustered. "I, um..." I don't want to lie. "I did have a... long journey." *Through time, that is.* "This is all strange to me." I indicate the pile of corn, the chickens, the tidy sisters sitting so gracefully on their blankets.

"Of course it is," Tía Dolores breaks in soothingly. She puts aside a husked ear of corn and brushes silk from her lap. "And you must have been captured very young. I have heard that *cautivas* taken from their families as children often remember little of their early life with their families."

"And besides, you hit your head," Josefina puts in. "That might be affecting your memory too."

The others nod agreement, their faces concerned.

Josefina tilts her head. "Can you remember which Indians captured you? The Apaches, perhaps? Or the Comanches? Did they live in tepees or—"

Suddenly, the pieces fit together. They think I was captured from my family, who would be Spanish, like them, and that I've been living as a captive with a group of Indians ever since. And Teresita—the same thing must have happened to her a long time ago, but in reverse. She was a Navajo Indian captured by the Spanish.

"We must tell Josefina's papá," Tía Dolores says firmly. "He will need to inform the officials in Santa Fe that we've found a *cautiva*. We will ask him also if María may stay here until we can find her relatives." She stands up. "Come, María."

Tía Dolores reminds me of my favorite teacher, Mrs. Burton from second grade. She had that same way of talking, take-charge but not bossy. She always knew just what to do—and I bet Tía Dolores is the same way.

Josefina bounces up also. "May I come too, Tía Dolores?"

"You may. I believe your papá is outside saddling his horse." Tía Dolores smiles at both of us and leads us out of the courtyard and through the big front gate.

A tall man is lifting a saddle onto a light tan horse

with a black mane and tail. He wears a hat with a wide brim, kind of like my grandfather used to wear when he was hiking. His face is lined and serious.

"Andres, may we speak a moment?" Tía Dolores says. Her voice is low and respectful.

"Yes?" Señor Montoya answers. "Do we have a visitor?"

"This girl's name is María," Tía Dolores says. "Josefina found her wandering outside." She quickly explains that I seem to be a *cautiva* who was taken so young that I don't remember much of my early life.

Señor Montoya studies me with grave eyes, and I look down. Out of the corner of my eye, I see Josefina standing beside me with her hands clasped in front of her and her head bent. I mimic her and say nothing. I have the feeling that I'm not supposed to speak unless someone asks me a question. I remember reading that in the old days, they would always say, "Children should be seen and not heard." It seems like Josefina's family follows that rule, too.

"You are welcome here, María," Señor Montoya says, and his voice is kind. "I will notify the Santa Fe officials and make inquiries to see if anyone knows of a family whose daughter was taken years ago."

My ears perk up at the words "Santa Fe." I *am* somewhere I know. Just not in the time I know.

Señor Montoya goes on. "I will send Miguel and some other men to check the hills. The *rancho* is not safe if enemies are nearby. In the meantime, you must stay here with us. We will find a home for you, if we cannot find your family."

"Oh! Um..." I stammer. This family I don't even know is going to all this trouble for me, and now they're going to be searching for an enemy that doesn't even exist. "Ah... my journey has been a long one." I choose my words carefully. "I'm very far from where I started. I don't think there are any enemies nearby."

Señor Montoya raises his brows and looks at me more closely. I hastily cast my eyes down.

"Nonetheless," he says, "the area must be checked."

Josefina gives me a sideways smile and reaches out to squeeze my hand.

Señor Montoya notices, and the corners of his mouth twitch up. "I see that my youngest daughter will take good care of you." He glances at Tía Dolores and she smiles back, her own eyes twinkling.

"Yes, Papá," Josefina says, her eyes still on the ground. "Thank you, Papá."

That's all she says, and as her papá swings up onto his horse and trots away, I think of how Dad and I talk and argue and laugh together at home. It's different here, but it seems like Josefina loves her father the same, even if she doesn't talk to him in the same way.

Josefina gives me a warm smile. "I'm so glad you'll be our guest, María! I've never had a girl my own age to stay before. It's like having another sister!"

❋ *Turn to page 22.*

he sun is low in the sky, and a hint of chill has flavored the air by the time we return to the courtyard. The delicious scent of frying wafts from the kitchen. After Josefina and I have hauled in our heavy baskets and dumped out the squashes, I sit on one of the blankets and help Josefina, Clara, and Francisca slice them into round disks. Then they show me how to string the slices with a needle and thread into a kind of really big squash necklace, which they call a *ristra*. Then they'll hang the *ristras* to dry—sort of like making dried apple slices, I guess.

"So much squash!" Josefina rejoices. She lifts one of the *ristras* high so that the end just touches the ground.

"So much water-carrying from the stream!" Francisca says. "My head aches just at the thought of it." She puts her hand delicately up to her forehead.

Why would her head ache from carrying water? I wonder. Maybe she thought about it too hard? Then I remember the servant with the water jug that we saw earlier.

"You'll be glad of these dried squashes this winter," Clara retorts. "We all will."

Tía Dolores appears in the kitchen doorway and

comes over to inspect our work. "My nieces are keeping their hands busy, as God intends," she says, smiling at us approvingly. "After all—"

"The saints cry over lost time!" Josefina interrupts, and she, Clara, and Francisca laugh. Their merriment is infectious, and I laugh too.

"I'm glad to see I've taught you well," Tía Dolores says with a twinkle in her eyes.

I sit quietly, thinking. At home we can get anything we want, all year round, just by driving to the supermarket. But it seems like Josefina's family wouldn't have enough to eat if they didn't grow and dry these vegetables. It must be hard work, hauling water in the heat of a desert summer, but they don't seem unhappy.

Francisca holds a small squash up behind her ear. "How do I look?" She tosses her glossy black hair. "Should I wear this to the harvest *fandango* tomorrow?"

A *fandango*—a party! My ears perk up. I do love parties.

Clara sighs and yanks the squash away. "Francisca, be serious. Squash *blossoms* in your hair, perhaps. But that's our food, not decoration."

"She's *wearing* the squash instead of *giving* the squash!" Josefina cries, and she and Francisca burst into laughter.

Josefina sees my confusion. "When a young lady wants to refuse a marriage proposal from a gentleman, her family sends his family a squash!" she tells me.

What a funny custom! I can't help laughing too, but seeing them all together, their heads almost touching as they murmur to one another, gives me a pang for Danielle. I want to whisper and laugh with my best friend.

As I pick up my *ristra* again and get back to work, Audrey's face swims up in front of me. *A new friend.* I push the image away.

❋ *Turn to page 63.*

We walk farther and farther from the house, skipping over tiny streams, skirting boulders, watching black ravens wheel and call to one another far above our heads. Sombrita bounds up a steep boulder. I stare up into the sparkling blue depths of the sky. Pine-scented air tingles my nose. Bright yellow cottonwoods cluster along the streams. My nervousness ebbs away. No enemies in sight. And I haven't spotted a single horny toad—yet.

"Mmm!" Josefina breathes in and closes her eyes. "*Piñón* is my favorite scent! Don't you love it, María?"

"It smells delicious," I agree, and together we close our eyes and inhale at the same time. "Mmm!" We open our eyes and giggle at each other.

"Sombrita! Stay close!" Josefina calls to the little goat, who is wandering into some bushes. She kneels down as Sombrita runs back to her. "You must stay near, little one," she says gently, looking into the goat's face. "There are dangers out here." She pats Sombrita firmly on the head and rises.

"I have to teach her," Josefina explains. "She's never had a mother to show her how to be a proper grown-up goat, so I try my best to do it."

"What happened to her mother?" I ask, struggling behind as Josefina strides up a rise. Small pebbles have collected in my moccasins, and the sun is hot now, baking the top of my head.

"She died giving birth to her." Josefina stops walking and rests with her hands on her waist. "Maybe that's why I feel so strongly that I have to help her. She doesn't have a mother . . . and neither do I."

I inhale. "Where—where is your mother?" I almost don't want to hear the answer.

"She died. Two years ago." Josefina looks toward the horizon, and I sense that she doesn't want me to say anything else. So I stay silent, but after a moment I reach out and squeeze her hand. She doesn't look at me, but squeezes back and swipes a wrist under her eyes.

We start walking again. After a few moments, I ask, "So . . . how did Sombrita survive after her mother died? Wouldn't she starve?"

Josefina smiles, though her eyes are still shiny. "Papá gave me a pouch of milk, and I taught her to suck it out through a rag in the top. That first night, I slept with her by the hearth. I kept her warm and fed until she was stronger."

I think of Fern feeding Wilbur the runty pig with a baby bottle in *Charlotte's Web*. "I've heard you can do that with baby animals. It must have been fun to take care of her."

We top the small rise and stop to look over the dry, brushy landscape. "It was," Josefina agrees. "But it was more than that, too. I just felt like I *had* to. And now Tía Magdalena—that's my godmother, Papá's older sister—is teaching me so that I can become a *curandera* like her, one day."

I must look confused because she clarifies, "A healer— Oh, here!" she breaks off. "I see rabbit brush over on the next rise." She points to a gentle slope where clusters of small shrubs are bursting with mustard-yellow flowers.

We hike over and set down our baskets. Josefina begins plucking the flowers and stems. A short distance away, Miguel gathers twigs and small sticks— I imagine for kindling—while Sombrita wanders through the low brush, munching leaves. Tentatively, I twist off a few flowers, trying not to mangle them, and drop them into my basket. "Mamá always loved autumn," Josefina says, her hands working quickly. The wind blows brown tendrils of her hair across her face. "It was her favorite season. She always said that the colors are giving us their last show before they go for their winter's rest." She holds up a rabbit-brush flower against the blue sky. "Look, María! Look at this yellow against the blue."

I gaze up at her strong, tanned hand. In the crystalline air, the yellow vibrates and glows against the jewel-like blue. It almost hurts, the colors are so brilliant. My breath catches. "It's beautiful." Then my eyes drop to Josefina's face, and I watch as she sweeps her gaze around the landscape. Her face is alight.

She loves this land, I think. *She loves it like I love Chicago.* This is her home. And I guess it's mine now too, sort of. Maybe someday I'll love it like Josefina does. But right now, the spiny stems of the rabbit brush have pricked my palm, and I bring my hand to my mouth to cool the sting.

Josefina notices my grimace. "Here, María, pick them lower down, to avoid the spines."

"Right." I watch her deftly pick a couple of flowers. "You know so much about all this—gathering the plants, how to find them. And how to weave, and how to make these into dyes for the yarn."

Josefina pauses, her face surprised. "I never thought of it that way. Gathering plants for dyes and weaving—that's nothing special. I'm not good at organizing the household, the way Ana and Tía Dolores are. And Francisca knows how to choose the most beautiful colors for weaving, and Clara always weaves so smooth and tight... I'm just learning, really, María."

I raise my eyebrows. "Well, it doesn't seem that way to me. You can be *my* teacher."

Josefina's round face crinkles into a smile, and she seems to grow a few inches taller.

❋ *Turn to page 67.*

hat else do you do for fun?" I ask the sisters, to distract myself from feeling guilty about Audrey. "Do you go to…"

I realize that there isn't really anywhere to go. No malls. No movie theaters. No TV, of course. What do they do for entertainment—visit the horny toads?

"Oh, we have plenty of fun times," Josefina says. "Tía Dolores has brought so many new things from Mexico City. She has a *piano*!"

She says this as if Tía Dolores has a pet giraffe. But I nod vigorously anyway. Pianos must be pretty special around here.

"We can show it to you tonight, if you like. Tía Dolores might play for us." She looks toward her aunt, who smiles. "I'm learning to play too, but I'm not very good," Josefina goes on. "We dance too—and we are learning to read and write! We've been studying with Tía Dolores for almost a year now." She looks very proud, and so do Clara and Francisca.

My mouth drops open, but I shut it with a snap. I don't want to embarrass them. But… Josefina and her sisters are just now learning to *read*?

Get ahold of yourself, I tell myself sternly. This is

a different time. Obviously, they don't go to school. They're busy growing their own food, for heaven's sake!

"There are important tasks too," Tía Dolores says in her brisk way. "Your lessons with Tía Magdalena will one day benefit the whole household."

Josefina must see that I don't know what Tía Dolores is talking about, because she explains. "I've been studying with Tía Magdalena. She's Papá's older sister who lives in the village. She's teaching me to be a *curandera*."

Clara leans over. "A healer," she whispers.

"Oh yes." I nod my head as if I've just remembered.

When we've strung the last sliced squash, Josefina and I carefully carry the *ristras* over to pegs on the wall of the courtyard. Other squash *ristras* are hanging there, already dried. Josefina takes these down and motions for me to hang up the fresh ones. Then we carry the dried *ristras* through one of the other doorways to what I assume must be a storeroom. I can glimpse barrels and bins standing against the walls. This must be where they keep some of their food. Josefina hangs the *ristras* on wooden pegs on the walls.

I follow Josefina through the courtyard into another

large room. It must be the kitchen, but it doesn't look like any kitchen I've ever seen. A big *adobe* fireplace is along one wall, with jars and baskets arranged on a low shelf beside it. Over the fireplace is a long, broad shelf that looks like a bunk bed. A ladder leads up to it and blankets are arranged on top. It looks like someone sleeps there sometimes. A long wooden table is loaded with melons, peppers, and onions in pottery bowls. The air is hot and smells of spices and roasting meat. Carmen, the cook, is bending over the fireplace, stirring something in a big iron pot.

Ana is kneeling on the floor, rubbing some kind of heavy-looking cylinder-shaped stone over another big flat stone. She's smushing a yellow, grainy powder, and it takes me a minute to realize that she's grinding dried corn kernels. She works fast, but the stone must be heavy, because I can see sweat beading at her temples and cords standing out on her forearms.

She smiles at us as we appear in the doorway. "You must be hungry, María. It won't be long until supper. I'm almost ready to make the *tortillas.*"

I don't see how she's going to make *tortillas* out of yellow flour anytime soon, so I resign myself to a long wait. "Soon" must mean something different in Josefina's world.

Ana dumps the flour into a bowl and pours in a thin stream of water from a jug. With her fingers, she mixes it all around, and before I even realize what she's doing, she's made several little dough balls. She flattens these out and lays them on a griddle with legs, which is standing over some glowing coals that have been raked out of the fireplace. After a moment, she lifts the little golden *tortillas* off the griddle and piles them on a plate. The whole operation has taken about two minutes.

My mouth is almost hanging open, I realize, and I shut it with a snap. If only Dad were here! Ana could give him a few lessons in New Mexican cooking.

Ana stands up with the full platter. "It's time for our supper," she says.

As she speaks, my stomach gives a loud gurgle. The sisters look at each other and try to hide smiles.

"We must feed our visitor," Josefina says, looping her arm through mine and giggling. "I can hear that your *belly* demands it!"

❀ *Turn to page 68.*

We continue picking, and soon our baskets are almost full. Then I hear a faint bleating coming from behind a stand of prickly bushes, just below us as the land slopes downward. *It's just Sombrita playing,* I think, and I pluck another flower. But something sounds different about her bleating, and I realize that Josefina hears it too. She stops, her hand still on a flower, her whole body listening. Miguel is at the bottom of the slope, breaking up a large branch.

"Something's wrong," Josefina whispers. For an instant, we stare at each other with wide eyes, and then she whirls around, the bright flowers dropping from her hand. We run toward the bleating, pushing our way through the prickly bushes that catch and snag at our clothes as if trying to hold us back.

Suddenly Josefina freezes, and I crash into her back. As I stagger to keep from falling, I see just below us a huge tawny cat—only three feet from Sombrita. The little goat is backed against a boulder and hemmed in on both sides by bushes.

She's trapped!

✵ ***Turn to page 72.***

I n what looks like a big main room—Josefina calls it the family *sala*—a fire is crackling cheerfully in the *adobe* fireplace in the corner. The sharp aroma of *piñón* smoke fills the room. A servant is loading a long, narrow table with platters of food. But there are no place settings, and there's nowhere to sit. I look around. Is the dining table hiding in a corner somewhere? But none is in sight. Maybe they eat standing up.

Francisca looks at me critically. "María, your sash is tied wrong. Come here and I'll fix it before we eat."

I look down. I've wrapped the piece of fabric three times around my middle, to keep the ends from trailing on the ground. "I wasn't sure—"

"Francisca!" Clara interrupts. "You are unkind to our guest. She's just being practical, aren't you, María?"

"Ah, I—"

"Practical! That's all you ever think of," Francisca shoots back, her hands on her hips. "A sash is supposed to be beautiful."

"It's supposed to help hold up your skirt!" Clara raises her voice.

"Well, *I* think María's sash looks both lovely and practical," Josefina inserts. She puts her arm through mine and lifts her chin, smiling cheerfully at both sisters.

"And I think our guest might appreciate washing up, girls, instead of bickering about sashes," Tía Dolores says, coming into the room with a bowl of cool water with mint leaves floating in it. She hands me a linen hand towel and a bar of lavender soap, and I quickly wash.

Delicate aromas reach my nose as I fold the towel and lay it with the bowl on a nearby bench. Some of the *tortillas* Ana made are steaming hot on a plate in front of me. I take the top one from the stack, only to realize that everyone else is standing around the table with their heads bowed. Whoops. They're going to say grace. I hurriedly replace the *tortilla,* hoping no one saw me, and bow my head too.

"Since your papá is still out with the sheep, I will say grace," Tía Dolores tells us. She says a short prayer, thanking God for the food and for the garden harvest. Her voice is low and soothing. I feel tension I didn't know was there leaving my body. When I open my eyes at the end, I notice that Josefina looks calmer too.

Everyone begins filling their plates with food.

"*Tamales,* María?" Clara says, as she hands me two from the platter. *Tamales!* They actually look just like Dad's.

"*Sí,*" I say, placing the little husk-wrapped bundles on my plate. "*Gracias.*" Dad would be proud of me. There is a bowl of mashed squash, some chicken, and a loaf of bread with a little cross pressed into the middle.

"Try Ana's special cheese," Josefina says, pointing out a bowl. It smells kind of funny, but the last thing I want is to offend my friend, so I spoon a little onto my plate and hesitantly take a small bite. It tastes strong and vaguely familiar—goat's-milk cheese! Just like the goat cheese Mom brings home sometimes. I flash on the goats outside. Wow, this must be made with milk from the family's own goats.

I wait for us all to sit around the table, but there are no chairs in sight. Everyone just takes a plate and sits on the *bancos*—*adobe* benches that are built into the walls. The squash smells delicious, but I don't have a fork—and actually, I realize, neither does anyone else. There are no spoons or knives either. How am I supposed to eat the squash? Then I see Josefina fold the *tortilla* at the side of her plate and use it to neatly scoop up a bite of squash. How handy—it's like edible silverware.

After we're done eating, a servant clears the dishes. Even through the thick walls, I can feel the evening chill. The single tiny window glows red and purple with the setting sun outside. But it's not glass—it's covered with a thin layer of some kind of luminous shimmery stuff, almost like...stone? I get up to move closer to the fire and examine the window on my way. Josefina is watching me. "It's a thin sheet of mica, to let the light in," she explains.

I think of the shiny rocks scattered around our New Mexico house. Dad told us that they were mica when we first moved in, and Henry and I marveled at how easily we could peel off thin shiny layers with our fingernails.

A cold draft blows in around the edges of the window, and I shiver. But here in the *sala,* the fire's warmth bakes my face. I wrap my *rebozo* more snugly around my shoulders as Josefina and her sisters settle on the bench close by.

❋ *Turn to page 73.*

osefina stifles a gasp. I press my hand to my mouth to keep from screaming. "What do we do?" I whisper. Miguel is too far away to help. I am sick with fear.

Josefina's eyes are wide and her face is desperate. She doesn't know what to do either.

"Let's grab her," I whisper.

"No, it's too dangerous!" With her eyes never leaving the mountain lion, Josefina bends down and scoops up a baseball-sized rock at her feet.

The mountain lion turns his head and glances at us. Then he fixes his eyes on Sombrita and crouches, ready to spring.

"We have to do something to save Sombrita," Josefina whispers hoarsely.

❊ *To tell Josefina to throw the rock,*
turn to page 77. ⌡

❊ *To grab Sombrita,*
turn to page 79. ↓

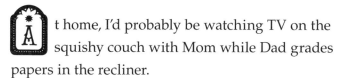t home, I'd probably be watching TV on the squishy couch with Mom while Dad grades papers in the recliner.

But Josefina's evening seems cozy, too. Tía Dolores has seated herself at the piano in the corner. With beautiful sweeping motions, she's playing scales up and down.

Josefina looks at me with pride. "Isn't it beautiful?" she murmurs. I nod, trying to look as if I'm hearing a piano for the first time.

Francisca is mending a torn shirt, and Clara has a large piece of cloth spread on her lap. She's using a big needle to embroider flowers all around the edges.

"That's beautiful, Clara," I say, bending nearer to admire it. I can hardly see it in the dim firelight, though. My hands itch to flip on a light switch.

Clara looks up and smiles. "Before your time as a *cautiva*, did you learn *colcha*, María?"

That must be the name of the embroidery. "Ah, no. I've never learned it," I say, careful not to lie.

"Mamá taught us *colcha* before she died." There's just the slightest hint of a catch in Josefina's voice.

"She was very good at it. She even made an altar cloth for the church."

"A flood damaged it badly," Francisca tells me, "but Tía Dolores helped us repair the *colcha*. We added bits of our own designs, too. I embroidered swallows on it—Mamá loved birds."

Clara nods. "Josefina embroidered flowers and leaves that Mamá loved, and I worked on sprigs of lavender—it was Mamá's favorite scent. Tía Dolores says that doing *colcha* keeps us close to Mamá. She loved to do it, and now we do too."

With the tip of my finger, I trace the outline of a flower on Clara's cloth. It makes me think of happy times. I see my room in our apartment back home. It's scattered with Drama Club scripts. Music soars from my speakers, and outside, the skyscrapers tower silvery gray against the blue sky.

Josefina's words float in through the image. "We can show you the altar cloth. We're keeping it safe here at home until next Christmas, when the church will need it again."

"Tía Dolores has helped us remember Mamá by making a memory book, too. It's a little book where she writes down poems and songs that Mamá used to love," Francisca breaks in. "Mamá was her sister, so Tía Dolores has many memories of her. Now we are learning to write in it too, so that we can remember things she used to say."

Tía Dolores turns from the piano, her *rebozo* drooping gracefully from her shoulders. The candles flaring on the wall send ripples of light up and down her dark red hair. She says, "Your mamá knew so many lovely poems and songs." Her smile bathes us in warmth, and I can see all four sisters lean in a little closer to her. Her eyes travel over each of them. "Words can keep special memories alive." She rises and gently caresses Josefina's cheek.

"I'll get the memory book!" Josefina jumps up. "It's lovely, María."

"Oh, I'd love to see it." This book sounds extremely special.

"Prayers are soon, girls," Tía Dolores cautions.

"We don't have much time," Josefina says, looking at me. "Should we see Mamá's altar cloth or look at the memory book?"

Words can keep special memories alive. Tía Dolores's

voice echoes in my mind. The memory book draws me strongly. But I want to see the altar cloth that brings Mamá back so vividly for Josefina, too.

❀ *To see the memory book,*
turn to page 80. ⤵

❀ *To see Mamá's altar cloth,*
turn to page 86. ⤵

o it," I whisper to Josefina.

Her eyes are steely. The mountain lion leaps. Josefina slings the rock at him, and he twists in midair like a spring. The rock catches him hard on the shoulder, and he lands heavily, scrabbling with his back feet for an instant. He stumbles, hesitates, and with one backward glance over his shoulder, lopes away, disappearing over the rise.

We both breathe a huge sigh of relief. Before we even have time to say a word, Miguel comes running up. Quickly, Josefina explains what happened, and once he sees that we are both unharmed, he tracks the cat down the hill to make sure he's really gone.

Josefina scoops up Sombrita in her arms, and we stand a long time, stroking the little goat, feeling her heartbeat return to normal just as ours do.

Finally, Josefina's eyes meet mine, and we burst into nervous giggles. "So much for a relaxing expedition into the hills!" Josefina says.

I place my hand over my heart. "That's okay. My heart needed a good jolt!"

Josefina heaves a big sigh and places Sombrita on the ground. "No more wandering off!" she instructs

the little goat. "María and I might not be able to save you a second time." The goat gazes up at Josefina with her yellow eyes, and I wonder if she knew how much danger she was just in.

"Do you want to go back to the house and rest?" Josefina asks me as Sombrita, unconcerned by her brush with death, nibbles at one of her moccasins. "After all, this was a lot of excitement on top of your long journey. Or shall we continue our gathering?"

As the adrenaline ebbs away, I suddenly realize how exhausted I am—between the trip through time and this brush with danger, I feel like I've been running for a week without stopping. I think longingly of the sheepskin bedroll in Josefina's room. But at the same time, we've barely gotten started on our collecting trip. I don't want to let Josefina down by not finishing the task we planned to do together.

❋ *To return to the house,*
   turn to page 88. ✓

❋ *To stay in the hills,*
   go to **beforever.com/endings**

I launch myself into the air, almost colliding with the mountain lion as he springs at Sombrita. For an instant, I smell his musky odor and feel the heat of his body. Then my fingers close on Sombrita's front leg and I jerk her toward me. The mountain lion screams, and a paw flashes out.

I see a burst of red as I pull the little goat underneath me. I can feel her heart pounding along with my own, and I squeeze my eyes shut, waiting for the mountain lion to leap onto my back. I flash on the part in *Little House in the Big Woods* where a panther jumps onto a horse's back and rips it up as the horse runs away into the woods. Now *I'm* the horse.

Something touches my back, and I scream.

✷ *Turn to page 83.*

"I'd love to see your memory book," I tell Josefina. She jumps up and leaves the room, and then comes back in a moment carrying a little book with soft brown leather covers.

Gently, I turn the pages while she looks over my shoulder. There are little drawings, handwritten poems, quotes. I think about how wrenching losing her mother must have been for Josefina.

Josefina points to a few lines written in careful script. "This is one of the first things I wrote down. It's a song I remember Mamá singing to me when I was a baby." She croons softly:

> Sleep, my beautiful baby,
> Sleep, my grain of gold.
> The night is very cold.
> The night is very cold.

She pauses, her face lit by the firelight. "Those are the very same words Mamá used to sing—and they are right here! Written down, so we'll never forget them."

She shakes her head, and I sense her amazement.

She doesn't have a picture of her mother, but she has this. She has her words.

"I remember that song!" Clara exclaims. "She would sing it to you in your cradle, Josefina, and we would all lean on her knees, listening."

Francisca's eyes are shiny. "I remember that too," she says. Her voice is muffled.

My own throat aches a little as I look at the sisters' faces. I've left behind a city I loved, but the people I love are still with me. You can replace a home, but not the people you love.

Josefina looks closely at me. "Would you show us what your old home was like, María? Will you draw it for us?" She turns to her aunt. "Tía Dolores, may we use a scrap of paper from the memory book?"

Tía Dolores flips through the pages. "Here, dears, this last page has an ink stain on it. Use this one." Very carefully, she tears the small page out and hands it to us. From the way they're acting, I'm guessing that paper is pretty rare around here also—along with water and pianos!

Josefina puts something into my hand. It's a big

feather with most of the feather part stripped off. The end is sharpened into a point. She puts a small glass jar of ink beside me. "Here, María. Show us your house."

❋ *Turn to page 89.*

expect blinding pain. Instead, I feel only Josefina's gentle touch on my back. Her voice fills my ears like the sweetest music. "María! He's gone! He ran away!"

"Are you sure?" Shakily, I push myself up. Amazingly, I seem to be fine except for a few scrapes. Then I look down at Sombrita, lying on the ground underneath me. My breath catches in my throat. "Oh, Josefina! She's hurt!"

The little goat lies still, her rib cage rising and falling rapidly. A deep gash gapes in her shoulder like a bloody mouth.

Miguel runs up behind us. "Stay with the goat," he tells us. "I'll track the mountain lion to make sure he's really gone." He trots off the way the mountain lion went.

Josefina and I drop to our knees over the little gray-and-white form. Blood seeps from the wound, staining Sombrita's soft fur and dripping onto the sandy dirt beneath her.

"We need to stop the bleeding," Josefina says. "Quickly, before she loses too much blood." She presses her fingers to her forehead. "Tía Magdalena never told

me how to do that, though. María, I don't know what to do." Her voice is starting to rise in panic, and I grab her fingers and pull them away from her face. I kneel down and look right into her eyes. I try to remember the way my drama teacher would talk down kids who were having an attack of stage fright.

"Josefina." I make my voice low and quiet. "You can do this. Remember, you knew how to save Sombrita when she was tiny? Now you can do it again." In truth, my heart is pounding out of my chest, I'm so terrified, but my voice is steady and calm. "You *do* have the skills. I believe in you."

Josefina raises her eyes and looks me in the face, as if searching for the truth there. She must see that I believe what I am saying, because her mouth hardens and her eyes suddenly glitter crystal clear.

"Leaves." Josefina speaks rapidly and points behind me. "Get me some of those mallow leaves. I don't know if this is right, but we're going to try."

Quickly, I grab handfuls of the broad, dark-green leaves sprouting from a low plant nearby. They're covered with soft hairs. Josefina layers the leaves over Sombrita's wound.

"Here!" I take off my *rebozo*. "Tie them on with this." Josefina nods, and twists the shawl into a bandage, wrapping it securely over Sombrita's shoulder and leg. Behind us, Miguel trots up. He nods when I look up at him, and I let out a breath. The mountain lion is gone.

Josefina strokes Sombrita's forehead and bows her own head. I can see her lips moving. She must be saying a prayer. I close my eyes too. My forehead is coated in sweat and my hands are trembling. I find myself praying, too. *Please let her live. Please let her live.*

❀ *Turn to page 91.*

"ill you show me the altar cloth?" I ask Josefina. A smile lights her face, and she jumps up from the bench and disappears through the doorway. In a few moments, she is back, carrying a folded white cloth in her arms. The sisters gather around, and Josefina gently shakes it out.

My breath catches. Richly colored flowers—crimson, indigo blue, golden—are scattered across the top and embroidered thickly around the edges. Green leaves sprinkled throughout make me think of a midsummer meadow. "You all did this?" I ask, tracing my fingertips around the tiny stitches.

Josefina nods. "We put our love for Mamá into every stitch," she says. I hear a little catch in her voice, as if she's holding back tears.

Tía Dolores looks over us all, sitting still, wrapped in our thoughts, and then she goes to the piano. Seating herself on the bench, she begins a quiet tune that winds through the room, swaying and rocking us with its melody.

After a few moments, the tune picks up speed, and Tía Dolores throws us a teasing look over her shoulder. She starts a rollicking dance tune. Josefina's face

lights up. The melancholy thoughts scattered, she takes my hands and pulls me up from the *banco*. Clara and Francisca dance together too, and we all spin with our full skirts flying out.

My heart is full, and somehow talking about what she's lost—and thinking about what I've lost—has made me feel *better*. "You know," I whisper to Josefina under cover of the music, "I think, after tonight, that I know my way home now."

Her feet slow and her hands tighten on mine. "Are you sure, María?"

I nod. Mom, Dad, Henry—they're waiting for me back in my own time. They've *been* waiting for me ever since we moved. Maybe I had to lose them first, before I could find them again. And I know where to look— my new Santa Fe home.

❋ *The End* ❋

To read this story another way and see how different choices lead to a different ending, turn back to page 76.

think I'm ready to go home," I tell Josefina.
"Are you sure, María?" Josefina asks, her dark
eyes concerned.

I nod, but even as I do, I wonder which home I mean.
Do I mean Josefina's home? Or my modern *adobe* house
with Dad and Mom and Henry inside? Or do I mean
Chicago—the only place that ever meant home before?

Then I realize, as Josefina and I make our slow way
down the sloping hills, with Sombrita springing ahead,
that when I told Josefina I wanted to go home, the image
in my mind wasn't the *rancho*—or Chicago. It was our
Santa Fe house, with the high desert surrounding it.

*I do see what Dad means about the beauty of the desert
now,* I think to myself as the sun slants low and golden
across the sky. This land seems different now—not just
too hot, too dusty, too empty. This is Josefina's home,
and she loves it—and now it's my home too. I wonder
if I can make a life here, the way Josefina has. It's time
for me to see. The first chance I get, I'll go back to my
own time—back home.

❋ *Turn to page 119.*

I picture our brownstone apartment building. I know every brick and crevice. I fumble with the quill and bend my head close to the paper. How do Josefina and her sisters see anything in this firelight?

Clumsily, I draw our apartment building, and the Chicago skyline behind it. After a few moments, I lay down the quill. "This is hard to draw with," I tell Josefina.

"But you have caught on quickly," she remarks, peering at the paper and kindly ignoring the many blobs and blots. I take another look at the drawing. Something that resembles a humpbacked mountain with a rectangle in front of it tilts across the paper.

Josefina tips her head. "Why, your home looks almost like *our* home. That looks like the mountains just beyond our *rancho*. See?" She points. "You've drawn one hill with a hump, just like the one outside."

"Really?" I look closer. Whatever I drew doesn't look like the Chicago skyline, that's for sure. Actually, it *does* look kind of like the hills around here.

"And these are the pine trees." Josefina indicates the little lines at the bottom of the page.

I squint. "That's supposed to be the fence outside our house."

"And there's the house right in the middle," Josefina goes on, as if she hasn't heard me. "How clever, María."

"*Gracias*," I say, staring at the paper. She's right. The rectangle looks like our modern Santa Fe home, and the hill could be the same one outside both my house and Josefina's. I started out trying to draw one home, and I wound up with another.

❋ *Turn to page 92.*

osefina opens her eyes. "We must get her back to the house, quickly. Miguel, will you carry her?"

Miguel lifts Sombrita as if she's a toy, and we start off up the slope. I can see the square shape of the house at the top of a hill a few rises away.

My heart is still pounding. I can't believe I've seen an actual mountain lion. "She will live, won't she?" I ask Josefina.

"I hope she will. I couldn't bear to lose her." The little goat's eyes are closed. She lies limply in Miguel's arms.

"Is she breathing?" I gasp, scrambling to keep up with Miguel's trotting. "She's so still."

Josefina rests her hand on Sombrita's ribs as we half-walk, half-run. "She is," she says with relief. "But her heartbeat is weak. We must hurry."

✻ *Turn to page 95.*

eñor Montoya appears in the doorway, and we all rise respectfully to our feet.

Tía Dolores gets up from the piano bench. "It's time for prayers, girls." I follow Josefina and the others to the back of the room, to a narrow table. It must be an altar because everyone kneels in front of it, with Josefina's papá in the center. Ana and Tomás, her husband, slip in at the back, and we all bow our heads.

Señor Montoya prays, and I let his deep, musical voice roll over me as I peek through my almost-closed eyes at the altar. It's covered with a beautifully embroidered cloth. Candles send wisps of smoke to the ceiling, and several brightly painted figures stand on their own special little platform at the back of the altar. They look familiar, and then I remember seeing some at the museum in Santa Fe. Dad told me they were figures of saints carved from wood.

I glance at the faces of the family gathered around me as Josefina's papá prays. They look peaceful, refreshed, as if they've all had a drink of cold water on a hot day. I get the feeling that this is a really important time of day.

I follow Josefina and her sisters toward the doorway after prayers are over. Tía Dolores and Señor Montoya are talking quietly by the altar. Then Señor Montoya says, "I need to check the animals for the night." He leaves the room.

"María," Tía Dolores calls softly, coming over to us. "You know there's a harvest *fandango* tomorrow night in the village. Josefina and her sisters will be going there in the morning to help prepare. Perhaps you'd like to join them."

"Oh, yes!" exclaims Josefina, before I can say anything. "You must, María! *Fandangos* are so much fun."

A party? Oh, this is the party they were talking about earlier. *Yes, please!* I open my mouth to say so, but Tía Dolores keeps talking. "However, Josefina's papá is going to Santa Fe for some business. He will talk with officials there and will also ask if anyone knows of a family in a village somewhere who has lost a child. You and Josefina may accompany him if you'd like, but you'll miss the *fandango*. I will go with you, and we'll take the wagon and stay overnight. If you decide not to go, Josefina's papá will go by horseback and will return for the *fandango* in the evening."

Beside me, Josefina claps her hands. "A party or a trip!" she breathes.

In my mind's eye, I see the downtown streets lined with shops, offices, and cars, and the cathedral soaring over everything. Of course, I know Santa Fe must look different in Josefina's time, but still . . . it's a city, right? It would be nice to have a taste of big-city life again, even if it's not Chicago. Already the empty black desert is pressing in at the tiny window in the *sala*. There are no sounds except the wind whispering around the *adobe* walls. A city! Streets! Buildings! People bustling around! Color, light!

I almost burst out, "Yes, I want to go to Santa Fe!" But then I waver. I love parties, and I haven't been to one for so long! My body almost aches for laughter and music. After all, I *am* kind of a party girl. I haven't felt much like having fun since we moved, but I do now— having Josefina as a friend must have perked me up.

✻ *To help prepare for the fandango,*
   turn to page 99. ✓

✻ *To go to Santa Fe,*
   turn to page 102. ✓

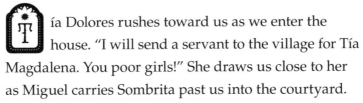

ía Dolores rushes toward us as we enter the
house. "I will send a servant to the village for Tía
Magdalena. You poor girls!" She draws us close to her
as Miguel carries Sombrita past us into the courtyard.

We follow Miguel as he gently places Sombrita on a
hide. Then we kneel over her anxiously to keep watch.
Her eyes are closed, and the *rebozo* is soaked with blood
where it covers the wound.

After what seems like an eternity, Tía Magdalena
bustles in, followed by Ana and Tía Dolores. We all
breathe a sigh of relief at her gray-haired, no-nonsense
presence. She nods at me, but there is no time for
introductions.

She deftly unties the crusted, dirty *rebozo* and, with
confident fingers, gently feels around the wound. The
gash is partly closed now, with the edges hardened and
the blood around it gummy. Tía Dolores sets a bowl of
steaming water at Tía Magdalena's elbow, and the older
woman pours in something that smells like vinegar
from a small jar she's taken from her pouch. Gently, she
bathes the wound over and over, until the blood and
dirt are washed away. Then she uncorks another small
jar and spreads a thick, strong-smelling salve over the

wound. "This will keep it from festering," she says, almost to herself. "It will heal without stitching." She hands a clean white cloth to Josefina. "Bind the wound tightly," she says. "You know how to do it well, I've already seen."

Her mouth pursed in concentration, Josefina carefully winds the bandage around the goat's shoulder, chest, and upper leg, just as she did with the *rebozo.*

Sombrita sighs. Her eyelids flicker and then open, just a little. "Look!" I gasp.

"Do you feel better, little one?" Josefina asks, stroking the goat's head. "You must lie still, to let your shoulder heal." She draws a second hide up over the goat for a blanket. Sombrita almost seems to understand her, because her body relaxes. She pushes her head against Josefina's hand and falls asleep.

We all let out a big breath. Tía Magdalena pats Josefina's hand. "You were right to bind the wound immediately, Josefina," she says. "Your instincts were correct."

Josefina's cheeks grow a little pink, and she nods. "*Sí.* I tried to think of what you would tell me." I can hear the respect in her voice. And she trusts

Tía Magdalena to guide her—I can see that.

Tía Magdalena smiles. "She will get well," she assures us all.

Ana gives Josefina a little hug, and Tía Dolores beams. "We're so glad," Tía Dolores says. Josefina leans forward and kisses Sombrita on the head, and I do too.

Josefina and I tenderly carry the little goat to a wide shelf above the fire in the kitchen. "She'll be warm here," Josefina says. "This is the shepherd's bed—it's not really a bed though. It's the warmest place in the house at night." A tender smile lights her face. "I slept with Sombrita here when I first took care of her." She covers the goat with a sheepskin. "Now I'll watch over you again, little one," she whispers, looking down at the little white head poking from the skin.

We sink down onto the floor and rest our elbows on the still-warm stone hearth. "I'm so tired!" Josefina says. I realize suddenly that I am too—more than tired. Now that all the excitement is over, a great weariness spreads over me. The kitchen is silent and peaceful with its neat rows of clay jars and stacks of pottery bowls. The firewood piled beside the oven gives off the woodsy scent of pine and smoke.

Josefina closes her eyes and rests her head on her arms. I close my eyes, and a sudden longing for home sweeps over me—but strangely, it's not our Chicago apartment I'm thinking of, but our *adobe* house, so much like Josefina's. My family is there, and I want to be with them. I think of the respect and trust Josefina has for Tía Magdalena and how Dad asked me to trust him that life in New Mexico will get better. Maybe I should, as Josefina trusts her elders.

We are silent then, as the minutes unspool in the quiet kitchen. Sombrita's breathing is slow and steady over our heads. She'll be all right now, I know. And I'll be all right. I don't know how I know that, but I just do. It's a sense I'm bringing back from Josefina's world—a feeling that love and trust are waiting for me. All I have to do is go find them.

I slip my other hand into my waist pouch. I squeeze the bird flute, feeling its smooth clay against my palm. It's time to go home.

❋ *The End* ❋

To read this story another way and see how different choices lead to a different ending, turn back to page 72.

'd like to go to the *fandango*," I tell Tía Dolores, a little shyly. I look over quickly at Josefina. Is that okay with her? Is she disappointed? But my friend grins. She doesn't look sad.

Tía Dolores smiles as if she understands. "It is good to have a little enjoyment every now and then, especially at the end of the harvest."

"Oh, good!" Josefina claps her hands. "And tonight you can sleep with me, María. It's late, and we must be up early for chores."

Tía Dolores gently traces the sign of the cross on Josefina's forehead, and then on my mine. Her fingers are soft and when she bends close to us, I catch a whiff of a lavender perfume. Then I follow Josefina out into the cold, dark courtyard. The sky is inky black and scattered with a million stars that glitter like diamond dust. I want to stand and stare and stare, but Josefina is leading me across the courtyard to the room where I rested earlier in the day. Clara and Francisca are already there, tucked into their sheepskin beds, and the room is warmly lit with a flickering candle in a sconce on the wall.

Josefina starts untying her sash and taking off her

skirt. I do the same, glancing around at the same time for some pajamas, or even a nightgown.

Josefina neatly folds her skirt and sash and tucks them into a trunk in the corner of the room. I do too. Then, still wearing her white blouse, she unrolls our bedding, folds back the blankets, and climbs in.

Okay. I guess they sleep in their blouses. I can't help wondering what Josefina would think of the purple-striped pajama bottoms and T-shirt I usually sleep in at home.

Josefina sits cross-legged in the bed. From a peg nearby, she takes down something that looks like a whisk broom tied together with a ribbon at one end. She unbraids her hair and starts running this broom through it, like it's a brush. Then I realize—it *is* a brush. Whew. Good thing I didn't ask her why she was combing her hair with a broom.

Josefina helps me comb out my braid and then I comb hers. She has lovely long hair that's wavy and curly at the ends, and the broomy brush does a surprisingly good job pulling out the tangles. Sitting in front of Josefina on her bed on the floor reminds me of sleepovers with Danielle. We'd sleep on the floor then too, in our sleeping bags, and we always did each other's hair. I liked a French braid the best, and Danielle usually wanted me to use the flat-iron on hers. I was a little worried I'd be homesick if I decided to spend the night in this world, but as Josefina blows out the candle and I snuggle down into the soft sheepskin, I feel almost at home.

❋ *Turn to page 103.*

í, *gracias.* I would like to go to Santa Fe very much, as long as Josefina does also," I say respectfully to Tía Dolores.

Josefina makes a little noise that sounds like a squeak and grabs my hand, squeezing it hard. I squeeze back, excitement bubbling up in me as well. Two girls, off to the big city!

I snuggle next to Josefina that night in her soft bed of sheepskins and wool blankets. Francisca's and Clara's quiet breathing fills the room, and cool desert air wafts in through the one tiny window over my head. Far away, a coyote howls. The sound still reminds me of a child screaming, and a brief chill runs down my spine. But my eyelids are heavy and the sheepskins are so soft, and I soon fall asleep.

❋ *Turn to page 109.*

I open my eyes to gray twilight. "Good morning!" Josefina cries as soon as I open my eyes. She's already up and buttoning her skirt over her loose white blouse.

Morning? It's the middle of the night! I push myself up and see the single small window glowing rosy with the sunrise. Ooof. They get up early here.

"We have a busy day, María," Clara says from the corner, where she is combing her hair in front of a small mirror on the wall. "We need to hurry and get the chores done so that we can go over to the village."

"I can't wait until tonight. Dancing!" Francisca says rapturously, closing her eyes and whirling around the room.

Clara frowns. "There's a lot to do first, Francisca," she chides her sister.

Josefina gives me a little sideways smile, as if to say, *There they go again.* "Tía Dolores fixed the tear in your skirt last night, María," she says. "She brought it in while we were asleep. Dress quickly. I need to fetch water from the stream."

I pull on the clean, neatly mended skirt and quickly braid my hair. Josefina and her sisters all put on the same clothes they wore yesterday, too. I guess when you don't have a washer and dryer in the basement, laundry is a bigger deal.

After Josefina returns with the water jug, there are more prayers at the family altar, and then bread and fresh goat cheese for breakfast.

We wave to Señor Montoya as he mounts his horse and sets off for Santa Fe, and then Clara, Ana, Tía Dolores, Josefina, and I all start off for the village, carrying baskets of squash, *chiles,* and even—*eek!*— dead chickens that will soon be turned into stew. Tía Dolores has a small basket of herbs. Francisca stays behind to take care of Ana's little boys and help Teresita, Carmen, and the other servants prepare food for tonight.

We walk briskly along the dusty road leading from the *rancho.* White clouds sail in the blue sky, and the crispy air is scented with wood smoke. Josefina and I trot to keep up with the others.

"It'll be so good to visit with everyone," Josefina says. "I haven't seen Señora Sanchez for a few weeks. She was my mamá's good friend. And the other women too—they all grew up with Mamá, and I've

known them since I was a baby. I remember falling
over a stool at Señora Sanchez's house and banging
my nose when I was just a little girl. They were getting ready for a *fandango* then too!" She smiles with the
memory. "The village is like a second home, really."

A powerful ache throbs in my middle. I'd like to feel
at home out here. I'd like this place to feel like it's part
of my skin and my blood, the way Josefina does.

We walk by plowed fields crowded with cornstalks
heavy with ripe ears. Pumpkin vines are growing
in between the green rows. A burbling stream runs
close to the path, and as we walk along, I can see that
little channels have been carved out, leading from the
stream to each field. A small wooden gate sits at the
opening of each little channel. Some of the gates are
lifted, and the water is running through those channels
into the field, and some gates are closed. Josefina calls
these little channels *acequias*—irrigation ditches. It's like
using a garden hose at home—except without the hose.
And the faucet. And any pipes, and a city water system.
But other than that, it's *just* like using a hose.

Women are kneeling at the edge of the stream. They
look up and call out greetings as we pass. Tía Dolores

stops to exchange a few words, and I watch a girl about my age scrubbing a shirt in the river water. She's using a handful of some kind of shredded-up plant as a soap, it looks like. Clean shirts and skirts and pants are spread on bushes to dry.

After about twenty minutes of walking, Tía Dolores calls back to me, "You can see the village now." I strain my eyes, expecting to see a bustling little town with shops, and people going in and out. But all I see are a few little *adobe* houses arranged around a square *plaza*. We must be getting near the village.

We walk right into the square of houses, and I realize that this *is* the village. Behind the houses are gardens surrounded by stick fences, and corrals for goats and horses.

That's it. Not a shop in sight. And the bustling crowds consist of a few women talking as they grind corn outside with the same type of stone cylinder and flat stone Ana used yesterday—a *mano* and a *metate,* she called them—and some boys playing some kind of a ball game with long sticks.

"Isn't it lovely?" Josefina says happily, looking around her.

"Oh, yes!" I try to match her enthusiasm. I don't want to hurt her feelings, of course, and it is cute. Just not very...busy. I'm starting to realize that there are just a *lot* fewer people in Josefina's world.

A girl comes up from the stream, carrying a basket of folded laundry. "May God grant you a good day, Montoyas!" she calls.

"And you, Ofelia!" Josefina calls back.

"Señora Sanchez's house is right next to the church," Clara tells me. She points to a small house with the door standing open. Lively chatter, delicious smells, and the sounds of knives chopping come from the doorway.

The church is made of *adobe,* just like the houses, but it's bigger and taller, and a bell is hung high above the door. It looks just like those really old churches Dad showed me in Santa Fe—but newer. The skin on the back of my neck prickles as I picture my own self in my jeans, standing in front of one of those old churches along with a bunch of other sightseers, reading a historical plaque. I really have traveled through time.

"Girls, Señora Sanchez is expecting us, but

I brought along some herbs to deliver to your Tía Magdalena," Tía Dolores says. "She's requested them from the *rancho.* Josefina, would you and María like to take them to your godmother? I can do it myself, though, if you're eager to join in the *fandango* preparations."

"María," Josefina says. "What would you like to do?"

I hesitate. The party preparations sound fun, but I want to meet Josefina's special aunt too. This might be my only chance.

> ✹ *To meet Tía Magdalena,*
> *turn to page 111.* 🗸

> ✹ *To go straight to Señora Sanchez's,*
> *turn to page 113.*

osefina and I are up with the sun. Josefina brings a jug of water from the stream, and after a quick breakfast of *tortillas* and goat cheese, we hurry to help Ana with the dishes.

"Girls! We are ready to go!" Señor Montoya calls to us from outside, and we wipe our hands on dish towels, kiss Ana, who is still washing, and run outside through the big wooden doors at the front of the house. Señor Montoya is standing there beside a wagon. Two mules are hitched to the front. I almost fall over. Of course— why would there be a *car* waiting for us? But for some reason, my modern mind had expected us to climb into the back of a *station* wagon and speed off.

The morning is fresh with a cool breeze left over from the night, and puffy white clouds sail high over- head like ladies holding their skirts up as they cross a room. The bright yellow wood of the wagon is cheerful in the brilliant blue morning, and the mules raise their heads when they see us coming. They look eager to go too. Tía Dolores is already waiting on the front seat. On the ground beside her, Josefina's papá smiles at us and extends his arm. "Ladies," he says with a touch of playfulness. Josefina giggles, and he helps her into the wagon, settling her on a board across the back with a blanket laid on top of it. Then he turns to me. "María, allow me to help you," he says.

I look at the mules, and at Josefina beaming at me from the wagon seat, and at Señor Montoya's strong hand and kind face. This will definitely be an adventure—and haven't I been missing the excitement of my old life? Here's some new excitement! Boldly, I grasp Señor Montoya's hand and haul myself up next to Josefina. Carmen hands up a bundle of food for lunch, Señor Montoya swings up into the seat beside Tía Dolores, the mules toss their heads, and with a jolt, we're off!

"Adiós! Adiós!" We wave to the entire family and the servants, who have all come out to see us off.

"Be careful!" Clara calls behind us.

"Bring us back something pretty!" calls Francisca.

❋ *Turn to page 120.*

"I 'd like to meet Tía Magdalena very much,"
I say. Josefina smiles as if she's pleased, and
Tía Dolores takes a bunch of dried leaves and stems
out of her basket. I follow Josefina across the flat,
hard-packed *plaza* and past the boys shouting over
their stickball game.

"I wish I could have played shinny when I was
younger," Josefina says as we pass them. That must be
the name of the game. It looks just like field hockey—
with even the same curved sticks. "But it's a game for
boys only."

We stop at the doorway of a small, tidy *adobe* house.
"Hello, children!" Tía Magdalena is standing at the
doorway to her house. She's gray-haired and wrinkled,
with eyes that crinkle when she smiles.

"Tía Magdalena, please allow me to present María,
a new friend who has come to us recently," Josefina says
respectfully, with her hands clasped in front of her.

Tía Magdalena gives me a sharp look that makes
me drop my eyes. It's as if she can see inside my head.
But she merely says, "Welcome, child. Come in."

We duck our heads below the low doorway of the
house, and immediately a pungent, dusty smell teases

my nose. Through a partly open door leading to a back room, I can see bunches of dried herbs hanging upside down from the ceiling beams. Suddenly I picture the shiny white aisles of the drugstore at home, packed with brightly colored bottles of every kind of medicine you could want. I realize that Tía Magdalena's house must be like the village pharmacy, and these plants are the medicines!

✸ *Turn to page 139.*

I really hope I get to meet Tía Magdalena some- time soon, but right now, I'd love to go join the *fandango* preparations," I tell Tía Dolores and Josefina.

Smiling, Tía Dolores waves us toward Señora Sanchez's, and heads for another little house nearby.

"Buenos días!" voices call out as we stand in the doorway. The little house is buzzing with activity. Some girls are hanging *ristras* of dried peppers, women are peeling onions and squash, and still others are making *tortillas* on a flat iron griddle over coals from the fire in the fireplace. Welcoming faces turn toward us, even as the women's hands never stop working.

I follow Josefina around the room as she greets each woman. They smile at us, and the older ones pat our cheeks. It's like a family reunion.

"My dear Josefina!" A comfortable-looking older woman bustles over to us, her apron dusted with flour. "I'm so glad you are here, and your dear sisters." She catches sight of me, and her eyebrows shoot up in sur- prise. "And you've brought a guest!"

Josefina introduces me to Señora Sanchez and quickly tells her my story.

"A *cautiva!*" Her eyes are tender, and she catches

my hand. "We are so glad you have returned, my
child. And we have much to keep you busy today!" She
laughs out loud as she looks around the chaotic house.
"Clara, Ana, I hope you will help me with the bread.
And would you younger girls mind little Luisa, Felipe,
and baby Mateo while we work?"

"Of course," Josefina says right away, and I nod.
I love baby-sitting—back home in Chicago, I'd just
started watching our upstairs neighbors' kids before
we moved.

Josefina and I herd the little boy and girl into the
corner. There, a baby lies on a kind of a small platform
lined with sheepskins. It's hanging from the ceiling
with ropes. The baby looks up at us with bright black
eyes from his soft bed. A strand of coral beads deco-
rates his fat little neck.

"Hello, little one," I coo, leaning over him.

"Play with us, play with us!" The other two crowd
around our legs, tugging on our skirts.

"*Sí, sí*," Josefina says, laughing. "María and I will
play with you."

I lift Mateo from the cradle and hold his soft,
heavy little body close to my chest. I hum him my

mockingbird tune. Felipe is clutching a carved wooden horse, and Luisa has a rag doll, with a lovely little dress and teeny braids. It reminds me of my favorite old doll, Clementine. She was a rag doll, too.

Josefina seats herself on the floor with the children and starts a clapping game with them, going faster and faster until they are screaming with laughter. It reminds me of the clapping games we always used to play on the bus, going on school field trips. I stand watching them, jiggling the baby as he slurps on his fingers.

Finally Josefina holds her hands up. "Enough!" she says, pink-cheeked and breathless from laughing. "Now I will tell you a story. Your mamá wants you to rest, I'm sure."

The children lay their heads in her lap, and I sit down and cradle the baby in mine so that he can listen to the story too.

"I'm going to tell you about *La Jornada del Muerto*— do you know that story?" Josefina asks the children. They shake their heads, their eyes fixed on her face.

"Well, you know that our trading caravans have to travel for many months across mountains and desert to bring us wonderful things from Mexico City,"

Josefina says. "And the desert is hot, and dry. Men have died out there."

Josefina pauses for effect. The children are perfectly still, their large eyes shining. I'm still too, I realize, and even the baby seems to be listening.

Josefina goes on. "One stretch of the desert has been especially terrible to the traders. It has no water, and some call the trail that runs through it 'The Route of the Dead Man.'" She widens her eyes dramatically, and Luisa gasps. "The first Spanish settlers crossed that desert long ago. At first, they drank just a little of the water they brought, to save it. But they became so hot and thirsty that they drank a little more. And then a little more. By the end of the second day, they had only enough water left to moisten their tongues. They thought they would surely die."

She stops, and Felipe pipes up, "Did they die?"

"Well," Josefina says. "The settlers had a little dog with them. The pup would range ahead of them during the day, seeing what he could see. But he would always return to camp at night. At sundown on the second day, he came back to camp as usual. But this time, he had mud on his paws. Mud! The settlers looked at one

another with hope in their eyes. If there was mud, there must be water. And they were going to find it.

"With the last of their strength, they followed him to a small spring hidden deep in the desert. They drank the water, which saved their lives and allowed them to continue their journey. From then on, that spring was called *Los Charcos del Perillo* so that people would always remember him," Josefina finishes.

The Pools of the Little Dog, I think. *What a good name.*

We are all quiet an instant, and then Luisa bursts out, "That was a good story!"

"Good, good!" her brother echoes, jumping up and clapping his chubby hands.

Josefina smiles and smooths her hand over the tops of their heads. "I'm glad you liked it," she says. "Now it's time to play quietly with your toys."

The children begin making a stable for the horse out of corncobs, and I turn to Josefina.

"They loved that story—actually, *I* loved that story too." I pause. "You're good with them—I should take lessons from you on caring for children."

Josefina smiles and holds her arms out for the baby. "I learned that story from Mamá. All I have to do is

close my eyes, and I can hear her telling it."

I pass Mateo over to her and let my eyes wander around the room. The women are all talking together as they work. Their laughs are those low, familiar ones you hear with people who've known one another all their lives. Outside the small window, I can hear the shouts of the boys as they play a ball game.

Josefina sits peacefully, rocking the baby and humming. She looks utterly content, as comfortable here as at home, surrounded by people who love her. I swallow and pretend to be folding Luisa's handkerchief, which has fallen to the floor. I see myself walking through the crowded halls at school, alone, and sitting solitary on my rock outside the house. People are around me all the time, but I still feel so alone. I wish I could bottle some of what Josefina has here and take it back to my own time with me.

❋ *Turn to page 124.*

he last thing I hear is the trilling notes of my flute, and then everything goes black.

When the blackness lifts, the sun is still hovering just above the horizon, flooding the rocks and sage and *piñón* trees with golden light. Daisy raises her head from gnawing at her paw and laps my hand as if to say *Welcome back.* In the house, I can see Henry holding the paper he's pulled from his backpack, and Mom and Dad bending over it. It's the same moment as when I left. But yet . . . it feels different. Almost as if I've brought some of Josefina's love for this place back with me. I can see it through her eyes now.

I climb down off the rock, and Daisy slips down beside me. I survey the distant hills with my hands on my hips. The three rounded spires point to the sky. Maybe Dad will hike to them with me tomorrow. I have a feeling this desert has a lot more adventures to share. I'm ready to find out what they are.

❋ *The End* ❋

To read this story another way and see how different choices lead to a different ending, turn back to page 26.

Three hours later, I'm hot, cramped, hungry—and still in the wagon. The wagon wheels squeak so loudly that conversation is difficult, and a fine layer of yellow dust has settled over everything and everybody. Rocky hills roll by endlessly, with small, glinting rivers winding their way around the bases. *Piñón* trees. Small *adobe* houses with stick fences like Josefina's. Then, bigger hills—mountains, actually—green and gold and touched with snow at the tops. They look cool. But I'm not.

I'm done with being jolted on the rutted road so hard that the top of my head feels like it's going to come loose. Even the cold *tamales* we've eaten for lunch don't refresh me. I think longingly of zipping into downtown Santa Fe in our car—a quick fifteen minutes, with air-conditioning.

But Josefina and Tía Dolores don't seem to mind the hot, bumpy ride at all. In fact, Josefina leans close to me and chatters on, pointing out landmarks here and there.

"María," she says now, "wait until you see the marketplace in Santa Fe! *Everyone* is there, and you'll see so many things to trade. And we'll visit with Abuelito and

Abuelita. It's been so long since I've seen them!"

She's practically bouncing up and down on the seat. It's pretty clear that Santa Fe is the most exciting place she's ever been. And her excitement is catching. I can feel my heart beating faster as at last Señor Montoya announces that we're not far away.

Already we're seeing more people on the road: other wagons, men on horseback, people walking with bundles on their backs, and big carts drawn by teams of oxen. Their wheels are incredibly squeaky, so loud that I want to cover my ears with my hands. Josefina mouths something at me, but I can't hear her over the racket of those squeaky wheels! I lean closer.

"There are a lot of people on the road because it's market day," she says.

I peer eagerly through the clouds of dust billowing around us. Then Señor Montoya shouts, "Whoa!" and the mules halt. The dust settles. We're at a crossroads. The traffic is flowing down the main road, but a smaller road branches off to the right.

Señor Montoya turns in the wagon seat to face us. "Girls, I'm taking Dolores to her parents' house now.

She wants to visit with Abuelito and Abuelita while I go to the *plaza* to trade and speak to the officials about María."

Tía Dolores twists around also. "Your grandparents will be eager to see you, Josefina. But it's up to you girls—you may go to the house with me now. Or you may go to the *plaza* first and join us later."

Josefina's forehead creases. "Oh, I want to visit with Abuelito and Abuelita! But... it's been so long since I've seen the *plaza*! Will Abuelita be disappointed if I don't come to visit with her right away?"

"She may," Tía Dolores says gently. "You know that she has strong opinions about how young ladies should behave. But you have traveled all this way. I know that you are looking forward to the market."

"Oh, I can't decide." Josefina wavers. "María? What would *you* like to do?"

"Um...um," I stammer. I don't want to get Josefina in trouble with her grandparents, but I'm dying to see the market she's been talking about, all the people and the trading in the *plaza*. And Josefina doesn't want to miss it either, I can tell.

On the other hand, the thought of getting out of

the hot sun, washing up, and getting something to eat is beyond tempting. And I'm really curious to meet Josefina's *abuelito* and *abuelita*. Josefina has told me that her grandfather tells the best stories she's ever heard.

❋ *To visit Abuelito and Abuelita,*
   turn to page 126. √

❋ *To go with Señor Montoya to the plaza,*
   turn to page 132. √

T he cooks have made a huge stack of *tortillas,* and Señora Sanchez's house is tidy as a mouse's hole, as my grandmother used to say. We all eat a quick meal of stew, and then Tía Dolores announces that it's time to return home for the *siesta.*

The white-hot sun is overhead now and seems to bore a hole straight into my skull as we trudge back along the path back to the *rancho.* The freshness of the morning has worn off, and even the bushes at the side of the path look dusty and tired. Sleeping through the hottest part of the day sounds pretty good in a world without air-conditioning.

But then my thoughts start to turn from sleep to the condition of my stomach. I'm starting to feel kind of queasy. As we keep walking in the blazing sun, I feel worse and worse. Oh boy. My stomach is definitely feeling bad. I think back to the stew I ate, and I almost groan out loud. No one else notices, but Josefina looks over at me quickly and takes my arm. "Are you well, María?" she murmurs, and I just shake my head.

When we finally reach the Montoyas' house, I head straight for the sleeping *sala* and collapse on the bedroll

Josefina spreads out for us. The other girls lie down
too, and soon the room is filled with peaceful breathing
as everyone takes a nap. But I can't sleep. Instead, I just
lie there, nausea rolling in my stomach.

❋ *Turn to page 129.*

'd like to go with you," I say to Tía Dolores. "If that is all right with you, Josefina."

"*Sí*, of course," Josefina says right away. Her face is lit up with the anticipation of seeing her grandparents.

At a large *adobe* house on the outskirts of the city, Señor Montoya halts the mules and helps us down from the wagon.

"Andres, what is this lovely surprise you've brought? We were expecting you alone, and now look at this—three beautiful flowers to brighten our *sala*!" A cheery-looking older man with a big gray mustache hurries from the doorway. "My beautiful daughter." He kisses Tía Dolores and takes Josefina's face in both his hands. "And my littlest granddaughter. You are even more beautiful and grown-up than the last time I saw you."

"Papá, please meet our guest, María," Tía Dolores introduces me. I clasp my hands and bow my head the way I've seen Josefina do. Tía Dolores quickly explains my story, and Josefina's *abuelito* looks at me kindly.

"*Bienvenida*," he says, patting my head. "We welcome you to our house."

Their house is built sort of like Josefina's, with big

thick walls and a central courtyard with rooms surrounding it. In the main *sala,* an elegant gray-haired woman dressed all in black looks up from her sewing as we come in.

"Dolores! What a wonderful surprise!" she exclaims. "My dear daughter, you are covered with dust. Go wash immediately." This has to be Josefina's *abuelita.* Josefina has told me she bosses everyone around.

Josefina's grandmother looks Josefina and me up and down, as Tía Dolores explains who I am all over again. "You must wash also, children," she commands us. "And then we will have refreshments."

The cool water a servant pours into a bowl for us feels wonderful on my dusty face, and I leave some pretty impressive hand and face marks on the towel. Josefina looks refreshed also. When we join Tía Dolores and the grandparents in the *sala,* two cups of cool water with mint leaves are waiting for us.

"How was your journey, Dolores?" Abuelita asks her daughter. "Was the road terribly dusty?"

I straighten up. *Yes!* bubbles behind my lips, but of course I know enough by now not to speak until I'm spoken to.

"Not terribly, Mamá," Tía Dolores replies quietly. "And not too hot, either."

Josefina nods agreement, and I look from one to the other. What? Weren't we all in the same wagon? Or were they on a different trip?

Then I realize—Josefina and Tía Dolores *did* think the journey was dusty and hot and probably just as uncomfortable as I did. But they don't complain. What's the point? There's no other way to get from the *rancho* to Santa Fe. Besides, I've been in Josefina's world long enough to see that they just don't complain, not even when there's something to complain about. Except for Francisca!

❋ *Turn to page 168.*

 late-afternoon sun gathers in the corners of the room, and as a cool breeze blows through the tiny window, the others begin to wake up.

"It's time to dress!" Francisca sings, jumping up from her bed. She goes straight to the trunk and starts searching through the layers of folded clothes. "María, I have a beautiful skirt I can lend you. I think it will fit if we— What's wrong?" She stops rummaging and stares at me.

"Nothing," I try to say, but another wave of nausea rolls through me. "Ooooh." I lie back on the pillow with sweat beading my forehead.

Beside me, Josefina is awake too. She leans over me and feels my head, then my palms. "You're very pale, María," she says. "And your hands are clammy."

"I'm a little sick to my stomach," I confess. "But I don't want to miss the *fandango*."

"You can't miss it!" Francisca cries. "It would be terrible if you had to stay here sick, while everyone else is dancing and listening to lovely music."

Clara frowns at her sister. "Francisca, how can María go, when she can hardly get out of bed?" she says sensibly. "Be practical."

Francisca ignores Clara and pulls a blue-green skirt from the trunk. She lays the lovely soft fabric in my lap. "Look at this, María, and you'll be up in a moment! I'll lend it to you for the evening."

Josefina gently nudges both sisters aside and folds the skirt. "María, you certainly can't go if you're ill," she tells me, sounding as firm as Tía Dolores. "I'll help you feel better, though, don't worry." She climbs off the bed and disappears through the doorway.

Soon she's back, carrying a steaming bowl in both hands. "I made you a settling tea," she says, placing the bowl in my hands. "Tansy mustard. It's what Tía Magdalena always recommends for upset stomachs."

I lean over and sniff. *Whoa.* I can't help wrinkling my nose and backing away. Unlike the chamomile tea Josefina made me when I first arrived, this one smells like burnt rubber.

I don't know what to do. I want to take the medicine—and I don't. That smelly brew is scary, even though I know that Josefina is learning healing. But I'm dying to go to the party, and I'm sure I won't get better in time without treatment.

I look into Josefina's dark eyes. I want to trust her.

She's my friend. Then the room is thrown into sudden darkness as the sun sinks below the window, and a chill settles over me. I suddenly long for home, yet at the same time, I want to stay with Josefina. And my stomach still feels awful.

❋ To refuse the medicine and go home,
   turn to page 137.

❋ To take the medicine,
   turn to page 156.

'd like to go to the *plaza* with you, Señor Montoya," I say rather shyly.

Josefina squeals and squeezes my hand. "Oh, María, it's the most exciting place in the world!"

"Now, now, girls," Señor Montoya says. "I have a lot of business to do. You may go, but you must keep out of trouble." He gives us a stern look.

I nod hastily. I can't imagine disobeying anyone with eyebrows like that.

We drop Tía Dolores at the door of a big *adobe* house that looks a lot like Josefina's, and she waves as we disappear back into the dust cloud that surrounds the road.

Soon we see more and more wagons and walkers on the road. People leading horses and pack mules are so close on both sides of us, I can almost touch them. In front of us, a woman is carrying a crate of live chickens balanced on her head, and beside her, a man has a huge basket of peppers lashed to his back. The houses are crowded close together now, and they extend as far as I can see.

Then in front of us, I catch a glimpse of a broad open space lined with *adobe* buildings on all sides.

Señor Montoya calls back to us, "There it is, girls—
the Santa Fe *plaza*." He points across the *plaza* to one
of the long, low buildings with a wide, shaded
veranda that takes up one whole side of the square.
He tells me that it's the Palace of the Governors, where
the officials work. An *adobe* palace—I never imagined
such a thing!

"Isn't it wonderful?" Josefina breathes. Her eyes are
shining beneath the *rebozo* draped over her head, and
she clutches the wagon seat in excitement. "So many
people! You can see *everything* in Santa Fe—everyone
comes here."

There's something familiar in her words and the
expression on her face. Then I know—it's just how
I used to feel when I'd go downtown back in Chicago.

*Santa Fe for Josefina is like Chicago was for me—the
big, dramatic center of everything,* I realize. This is the
most sophisticated, modern place she's ever been.
Okay. I'm going to think that way too. I take a deep
breath, wipe the dust off my forehead—it's mostly
mud now, since it's mixed with sweat—and sit up
a little straighter.

We roll right up to the *plaza*, and I gawk. In an

instant, everything I thought about Santa Fe being sleepy and dull is blasted apart. There are so many people and so many things that I hardly know where to look. Chicago's Magnificent Mile has *nothing* on this place.

Josefina can see how wide my eyes are, and she points out the different people and sights as we drive around the edge of the *plaza*. I listen hard to her brief descriptions: priests in sober black robes, and people from the surrounding farms and *ranchos* leading goats, horses, mules, and oxen to sell. Cages of chickens rest on the ground, waiting for buyers, and dogs mill around the ankles of their owners.

Along one side of the *plaza*, horses are lined up. Men are walking around, patting their necks, examining their legs. "Those are horses for trade," Josefina says. "Aren't they beautiful? Maybe we'll go look at them later."

As our wagon rounds a corner of the *plaza*, Josefina says, "These are Pueblo Indians." She points out a group of people sitting on the ground, with melons, pumpkins, and apples spread out on a hide in front of them. Their hair is cut differently from

that of Josefina's family, with bangs straight across, and they wear white shirts with shawls draped over one shoulder. "Maybe we'll see Mariana, my friend. She lives at the *pueblo*. Her grandfather Esteban is Papá's good friend. They trade together."

Josefina gazes across the *plaza*. "Oh, look!" she says. "Here comes Señor García, who owns more land than anyone else."

I stare at the elegant man riding into the *plaza* on a bay horse. His saddle is mounted with silver, and he wears odd, tight pants of green silk that have buttons all the way up the leg. He's left half the buttons undone, though, so that his white stockings show. "I think he forgot to button his pants," I say, and Josefina laughs merrily.

"You *have* been away a long time, María! That's just the latest fashion. And there's one of the trappers!" She nods her head at what I first take to be a bear riding a burly horse. Then I realize that it's a man with a bushy beard and long matted hair, wearing clothes made from skins, and with a big pile of furs tied on the horse behind him. "They live alone in the mountains and hunt and trap for months at

a time. Then they come down here to trade their furs," she explains.

"Oh." I nod understanding. How could I ever think Josefina's Santa Fe was dull?

✹ *Turn to page 144.*

I set down the bowl of tea I've been cradling, without taking a sip. "*Gracias* for the tea, Josefina, but I don't think I can drink it right now. I should probably stay back and rest," I say.

"Are you sure, María?" Her dark eyes are troubled. "Do you want me to stay with you?"

"No, I don't want you to miss the *fandango* just because I'm sick," I say. "Go, and have a good time for me."

Josefina strokes my hand, her brow furrowed, and then sighs and stands. "Only if you're sure you're not very sick."

"I'm really okay. Just tired, mostly." I push myself up higher in the bedroll. "But you know . . . I think that I'm starting to remember some things about my family."

"Oh, María, that's wonderful!" Josefina beams and pulls the blanket up around me. She tucks in the corners and smooths it out. "Rest now. We must go, but Teresita will be here if you need anything."

"Josefina—" I catch at her hand as she starts to turn away. "I . . . think I remember where my home is now. I must leave you soon to look for it. But I couldn't have remembered without you. So, I wanted to make sure I told you . . . *gracias.*"

A grin spreads across my friend's face, and our eyes meet in a bond that I know will last me forever.

When everyone leaves, and the room is in darkness, I raise the flute to my lips and play the special tune. I'm going home.

❋ *Turn to page 147.*

osefina offers Tía Magdalena the herbs, but the healer shakes her head. "Come into the storeroom, and I'll show you how to put them away yourself."

She leads us into the back room. Here, the walls are bright white, and jars of all shapes and sizes line wooden shelves built along one wall. "Take one down," Tía Magdalena says, seeing me eye the jars.

I reach for a small brown jar, lift the lid, and peer inside. It's full of dark, red-brown flakes.

"Deer blood," Tía Magdalena says, and my head jerks up, my eyes wide. Josefina grins at me.

"It's good to help you regain strength after an injury," Josefina says. "You mix it with water and drink it."

I hurriedly replace the jar on the shelf. "Maybe next time," I say, and they both laugh.

Tía Magdalena shows us how to prepare the herbs we've brought. We strip the dried leaves from the stems and crumble them into small bits in a bowl. Then I scrape them into an empty jar, and Josefina caps it with a round wooden plug.

"Now," Tía Magdalena says, smiling at us, "you

are my guests and we must have some tea."

We settle ourselves around the scrubbed wooden table in the front room, and the *curandera* brews a pot of mint tea. It smells delicious, and I hold my cup out toward the teapot.

"What is this cut?" Tía Magdalena pours the tea and sets down the pot. She takes my hand and gently touches a wound on the back. I've noticed it, but I haven't thought much about it. I must have gotten it when I "arrived" here.

"It's nothing," I say. But the skin around it is turning red, and when Tía Magdalena touches it, it hurts.

"You must care for it," Tía Magdalena says sternly. "Josefina, do you remember how to make the vinegar soak?"

"Mix vinegar and water and soak a cloth in the mixture, and then bind the wound with the soaked cloth," Josefina answers.

"Very good!" Tía Magdalena's eyes crinkle and her voice is warm as she praises my friend. "Do you think Josefina will make a good *curandera* someday soon, María?"

I nod and smile, but Tía Magdalena gives me that

intent look again. "You are sad, my child," she says. She makes it a statement, rather than a question. "Tell me what's troubling you."

I look into her wrinkled face and then at Josefina's round, rosy one beside her. All of a sudden, all the tears I've kept back since we moved well up inside me. My throat swells and aches, and I can feel tears gathering at the corners of my eyes, threatening to spill. I know my face is going blotchy, the way it always does when I cry. I shake my head, not trusting my voice.

Tía Magdalena reaches out and puts her hand over mine. Her palm is warm and rough. The tears erupt. "I miss home," I weep, and I can't stop crying. I cradle my head in my arms and sob.

"María has been a *cautiva* until very recently," Josefina explains quietly to Tía Magdalena over my head.

"Ah," the healer says. Through my tears, I feel her callused hand stroke my hair. "Cry, child. Let the sadness flow out."

After a minute, my tears slow. I sit up, gulping. Josefina scoots over so that she is right beside me, and passes me a clean, folded handkerchief. I mop my cheeks. The cloth smells of soap and lavender. She puts her arm around me, and I lean against my friend's shoulder. I feel wrung out but peaceful, the way you do after a good cry.

Tía Magdalena dips Josefina's handkerchief in a bowl of water and bathes my face. It reminds me of the way my mom always wiped my face with a cold wash-cloth after I'd been crying when I was younger.

"It's a terrible thing, to lose one's home," the healer says. "It can break your heart apart."

Her words feel very true.

"I can't imagine having to leave the *rancho* and Papá and Tía Dolores and my sisters," Josefina says.

"And yet, you too know what it is like to lose something very precious." Tía Magdalena wrings the handkerchief out. "And even though you will never stop remembering your dear mamá, are you happy again, Josefina?"

Josefina looks a little surprised. "I suppose I am," she says, knitting her brows. "I hadn't thought about it that way."

"And you will be happy again too, María," the *curandera* tells me. "The healing power of time can be greater than any medicine I have in my storeroom."

I sit up and take a deep, wavery breath. "I feel a little better now, actually."

Tía Magdalena smiles. "And the healing power of tears should not be forgotten either. Feelings kept inside can fester like a wound."

We chat and drink the mint tea, and eat licorice-flavored cookies Josefina calls *bizcochitos.* The sun traces a path across the yellow wood of the table, and outside the window, swallows swoop and call to one another.

✱ *Turn to page 149.*

eñor Montoya parks the wagon in the central *plaza* and unhitches the mules, who look glad to be resting. While they eat feed out of nosebags, Señor Montoya takes some folded papers out of his satchel and looks them over.

I watch a settler setting up his trade goods just a few feet away. He is arranging stacks of blankets and strings of shiny, dark red *chiles* on a canvas cloth. He has small bags of some kind of nut, too. Josefina says they are pine nuts.

"Josefina!" a voice calls, and I turn around to see a dark-haired girl running up to us. Her heavy bangs fall almost to her eyebrows. She wears moccasins like mine and Josefina's, but hers are white, and she has a blanket draped over one shoulder and tied around her waist with a beautiful woven sash.

"Mariana!" Josefina greets her friend with a big smile. "This is María, who is staying with us."

Mariana has one of those smiles that makes everyone else feel like smiling too. "Come see my grandfather," she invites us. "He's brought some of the best pottery we've made this summer."

"That sounds fun," I say, but then a man steps up

beside us. By now, I can tell that he's a *patrón*, like
Señor Montoya.

"*Buenos días*, Señor Montoya," he says.

"*Buenos días*," Josefina's papá responds. "I hope
your harvest has been good, Señor Jaramillo."

"*Sí*, God has blessed us this year," the man replies.
"But there is a matter I wanted to discuss with you,
about the *acequia* near the edge of the village..."

As the two men talk with their heads close together,
we hear a voice calling. "Mariana!"

Josefina's friend turns to us.

"That's my grandfather! Shall I tell him you're
coming with me?" she asks.

I take a step toward her, but something else catches
my eye. Señor Jaramillo has a clay flute strung around
his neck on a cord. It's a bird too, but not as fine as
mine. It's smaller, and there are no wing or feather
markings.

"My friend María has a beautiful flute too," Josefina
tells Señor Jaramillo.

I look up, startled. I didn't expect Josefina to mention my flute. It's not that it's a secret, exactly. It's just
that I think of it as a sort of private thing.

"Do you?" Señor Jaramillo asks. "May I see your flute? Fellow musicians always like to see new instruments." He smiles, and his eyes are kind.

I untie the pouch Josefina gave me to wear at my waist and bring out my flute. He takes it in his hands and turns it over. "This is skillfully made, María. Finer, perhaps, than my own flutes." He pauses. "Would you consider trading it?"

"Oh, no," I say right away. But Señor Jaramillo has put his hand in his pocket. He pulls out a small blue rock. It's about the size of a quarter, and it gleams bright blue-green. Some parts are flat, and those surfaces shine cool and blue.

"Oooh," I gasp, and beside me, I hear Josefina catch her breath in delight.

"Turquoise," she breathes.

"The turquoise is not valuable, but it is beautiful, as you can see," Señor Jaramillo says. He holds the turquoise out closer to us. It glows in his hand like a piece of the sky fallen to the earth. With his other hand, he reaches for my flute.

❋ *Turn to page 151.*

B irdy!"
I open my eyes. I'm back on my boulder, and Mom is calling from the doorway of the house. Quickly, I sit up, brushing at my T-shirt as she comes over.

"I've been calling and calling," she says. "Were you asleep?"

"Um, sort of . . ." I clamber down from the boulder, and Daisy jumps down behind me.

Mom loops her arm through mine. "Well, let's go in. Dad's *tamales* are almost done."

"Yum," I say, and I realize I already feel better.

She shoots me a curious glance. "I thought you didn't like them, honey. I was going to offer to make you a chicken breast."

I think back to the clay platter on Josefina's table. The steam rising from the husk-wrapped bundles. The faces of Josefina, Clara, Francisca, and Tía Dolores, glowing in the candlelight—loving one another, loving their home.

"Well, maybe I've just realized that there's a lot to love here in New Mexico. More than I thought before," I tell her. We're at the house, and Mom opens the door.

The warm aroma of cooking billows out, riding on a wave of Henry's and Dad's laughter. "Maybe I just needed some time." Like nearly two hundred years.

❋ *The End* ❋

To read this story another way and see how different choices lead to a different ending, turn back to page 131.

We stay so long at Tía Magdalena's that we never make it over to Señora Sanchez's. Tía Dolores has to fetch us to go back home and rest before the *fandango*. She brings us a few *tamales* to eat on the way.

As we leave the little house, my heart feels lighter than it has since the day our moving truck pulled onto the westbound highway out of Chicago. It's amazing that just talking can make me feel so much better. It's like having healing power in your words, I think, as I walk down the dirt path beside Josefina. And all you have to do is notice when someone is feeling sad or lonely—and you can talk with them and help them feel better, just like Tía Magdalena did with me.

We walk quickly, eager to reach home, and my thoughts seem to keep time with our footsteps. I could even do what Tía Magdalena and Josefina have done—I mean, not heal people with medicines, but help them in other ways—just by listening when someone needs to talk. Even people in my own family.

I swallow then, suddenly ashamed of myself. Henry and Mom and Dad seem so happy with our move, but they've had big adjustments too. Even Audrey at school—maybe she's trying to be friends with me because she could use someone to talk to also. I just haven't been paying attention.

I suddenly realize how many times Josefina has noticed when I'm feeling tired or sad. She's lost more than I have, and somehow, she still manages to pay attention to others. And she actually seems to *like* it— it makes her happy. Maybe listening to others a little more and myself a little less would make me happier, too. I don't know—but at least I could try.

❋ *Turn to page 153.*

o!" I cry suddenly and clutch my flute to me. The spell is broken. My only link to home!

Josefina sees the distress on my face and quickly steps between me and the *patrón*. "We are not interested in trading. *Gracias*," she tells Señor Jaramillo firmly.

Señor Jaramillo looks at us narrowly but nods and moves over to Josefina's papá to continue the *acequia* discussion.

I'm breathing hard, and my palms are wet with sweat. "I—I think I should sit down," I say.

"*Sí*, let's rest by the wagon," Josefina says right away. "The heat and the dust are too much for anybody."

We walk slowly back toward the wagon and hoist ourselves up to sit on the seat, with our legs dangling. I bow my head and try to gather my thoughts while Josefina pats my back. I squeeze the clay flute tightly.

"Be gentle, María." Josefina delicately loosens my fingers. "You'll shatter your flute if you squeeze it so hard."

I look at the concerned face of my friend, who can see how distressed I am and who is so caring, even when she doesn't know exactly what's wrong.

Josefina, I wish I could explain, I think. *My link to home is more precious than ever now that I've almost lost it.* My *home* is precious, and my family. I love Josefina's world, but I want to go back to my own, I realize suddenly. I can see now how much it means to me—and how much I would miss my family if I couldn't see them again.

❋ *Turn to page 161.*

As soon as we return to the *rancho,* Josefina, Clara, Francisca, and I all curl up on our beds to rest before the *fandango.* When we get up, the sun is setting outside in a beautiful glow of dusky purple and fiery rose-orange. Black clouds are silhouetted against the horizon, and the air is soft and scented with pine and wood smoke. I feel the old party excitement rising, and Josefina and her sisters must feel it too, because Francisca is singing as she twists her braids up onto her head, and Clara is dancing with Josefina in a rare light-hearted moment.

"You must let me help you with your hair, María," Josefina offers. She sits me down on a chair and combs out my mussed braid, carefully untangling the snarls with her fingers. Then deftly, she braids my hair again neatly. "I'll lend you my blue silk ribbon," she says. I get the sense from the way she says this that the ribbon is a special treasure. She gets up and opens the trunk sitting against the wall. Digging carefully through the items inside, she pulls out a little bundle of white cloth. She opens it reverently and pulls out a sky-blue silk ribbon.

"*Gracias,*" I tell her, gently stroking the soft silk

between my fingers. I tie it at the end of my braid. Josefina pulls on a blue-green skirt and a fresh blouse. Then we stand back and admire each other in our party finery.

Tía Dolores looks in at the doorway. "Girls, it's time to go," she says. All talking and laughing, we head out into the twilight, full of the promise of the party.

Inside Señora Sanchez's house, the dancing has already begun. Ladies in full skirts trimmed with ribbons sway with gentlemen in short jackets. At one end of the room, a fiddler and a guitar player fill the air with a rollicking tune that reminds me a little of square-dance music. Candles flicker and flare on the walls, and in a corner, a table is spread with a cloth embroidered with flowers. A painted pottery bowl of flowers sits in the middle.

Francisca is whisked away immediately by a handsome young man, and Tía Dolores laughs and accepts an invitation to dance from Tomás, Ana's husband. My feet are tapping, but I notice that no one my age is waltzing. Instead, Josefina pulls me down to sit on the floor with her. All around us, other kids are sitting on the floor and crowded on the *bancos* with their

grandparents, watching the dancers and clapping
in time.

Dip-sway-three, one-two-three. I hum with the
music. "I think I could play this on my flute," I whisper to Josefina. I take the little bird from my pouch
and start to lift it to my lips, but Josefina gently shakes
her head "no."

I sigh. It seems like a *fandango* might not be as much
fun as I thought. Then Josefina leans over and grins.
"Let's go practice the dance steps outside," she says,
keeping her voice low.

I jump up right away, but just then, a wonderful
fragrance floats toward us. Señora Sanchez is putting
tortillas and a pot of chicken stew on the table. My
stomach is rumbling. It's craving food almost as much
as my feet are craving dancing.

    ✳ *To sample the tortillas and chicken,*
      turn to page 158.

    ✳ *To go outside and dance,*
      turn to page 173.

close my eyes and take a big swallow. Then my eyes open wide in surprise. It's not that bad!

After a half hour or so, the gurgling in my stomach dies down and the nausea dissolves. I laugh and hug Josefina, and we do a celebratory little dance. "You cured me!" I tell her. "All your lessons with Tía Magdalena have paid off."

"Oh . . ." Josefina brushes away my praise, but her cheeks are pink with pleasure.

Then Josefina and Francisca help me dress in a white blouse with lace flounces on the sleeves and around the neckline, and Francisca's beautiful blue-green skirt that flies out when I twirl. Josefina ties a long blue fringed sash around my waist, and Francisca tucks a bright yellow flower into my braid. They stand back to admire me, and Clara sighs. "You are beautiful, María. The skirt makes your eyes look green."

"Gracias," I say, trying to imitate Josefina's modest tone.

Tía Dolores and Ana join us. Tía Dolores looks beautiful in a dark red flowered dress, and Ana is wearing a black skirt with yellow bands at the hem. "My dear children, you look lovely," Tía Dolores says, her warm smile lighting her face. She smooths a stray tendril behind Francisca's ear and pats Clara's cheek. "Now, then, we're all ready! We must go—we don't want to be late."

A wagon, with two mules harnessed to it, is waiting for us. Ana's husband, Tomás, helps us climb onto the boards laid across the wagon box, while Tía Dolores sits in the front with Señor Montoya. With a jolt, the wagon starts, and we all set out in the sunset for the village.

❋ *Turn to page 164.*

Dancing sounds wonderful, but my stomach is calling louder. "Come! Eat!" Señora Sanchez calls to the room, and the musicians end their music with a flourish. The adults crowd toward the tables, laughing and talking with one another as they pile chicken stew and *tamales* on their plates. A gray-haired man with a big mustache is teasing Señora Sanchez. Josefina's papá helps an older man reach the *tamales.* Their faces are glowing in the candlelight. It feels like a family gathering, even though I know they're not related. But in another way, they kind of are—it feels as if everyone here belongs to one big extended family.

My stomach is gurgling, but I wait politely with Josefina, Clara, and the rest of the children for the adults to finish before we serve ourselves. I heap the delicious-smelling stew, which is full of squash, tomatoes, and peppers, onto my plate and add two *tamales* at the side. Clara and I crowd next to Josefina on a *banco*, set our plates on our laps, and eat quickly, filling our empty stomachs. All around, the other guests are laughing and talking as they eat.

At last, my plate is empty. I mop up the last bits of stew with a *tortilla*, then sigh and set down my plate on

the floor beside me. I'm perfectly content with my belly full and my friend beside me here in the bright, warm *sala. There's nothing more I want,* I think to myself—and then I realize that maybe this is a perfect time to leave Josefina's world. Maybe I can bring some of this peace I feel back with me.

I take a deep breath. "Josefina, I . . . I think it's time for me to go," I tell my friend. "Tomorrow, perhaps."

Her eyes widen with surprise and concern. "But María! We haven't found your family yet," she protests. "Where will you go?"

I put my hand over hers. The music has started again and the adults are dancing. The lilting notes swirl around us. I lower my voice. "I know. But . . . I just have this *feeling* that I'll be able to find my family. I . . . can't exactly explain it. It's just a sense I have that I might be able to find my way home now." I look right into her eyes. *I'll be able to find my way home in my heart,* I tell her silently.

Josefina's eyes narrow, and then she nods slowly. "*Sí,* I understand. I know that sometimes you just have to trust that things will be well. Even if you don't know why or how."

I squeeze my friend's hand. "But I do know one thing—I'm awfully glad I met you on my journey. It..." I hesitate, searching for the right words. "It's almost been like coming home. You and Tía Dolores and Teresita and Francisca and Clara—you all gave me the strength I need to find my way home."

"María...in case I forget to tell you in the morning ... thank you for being my sister—for a little while." Josefina's eyes are shiny.

I grab her into a hug. "What do you mean, 'for a little while'? I'll always be your sister." My throat swells and I feel my eyes getting wet. "Always," I repeat softly.

❀ *The End* ❀

To read this story another way and see how different choices lead to a different ending, turn back to page 94.

realize that Josefina is still watching me, her brows knit. I sit up straighter and swipe at the sweat on my forehead. "I'm all right," I tell her.

"Are you sure?" she asks, and I nod.

"In that case, why don't we go visit with Mariana?" We slide down from the seat of the wagon and cross over to Señor Montoya. "Papá, may we see Mariana?" Josefina asks quietly.

Señor Montoya nods. "Yes. Tell Esteban I will be over soon to greet him," he says.

"Come!" Josefina gives me an eager smile. We weave our way over to Mariana through the piles of goods displayed on hides, and past mules and bleating goats tethered together, waiting for new owners.

"Oh!" A rider with spurs on a big black horse crosses right in front of me. A rifle is stuck into a scabbard on his saddle, and a sword hangs from his hip.

"A soldier," Josefina whispers in my ear. "They travel with the caravans bringing goods from Mexico City, to protect them from bandits."

I follow Josefina over to a hide spread on the ground, where a gray-haired man is sitting calmly. His straight hair hangs to his shoulders, unlike Señor

Montoya's, which is cut short, and he wears a piece
of cloth tied around his forehead. His moccasins are
white, like Mariana's, and he wears a white shirt and
pants with a dark shawl over one shoulder.

Spread out before him are pottery jugs and bowls
in neat rows. They are made of smooth reddish clay.
I've seen jugs just like this at Josefina's house. I wonder
if her papá trades with Esteban for them.

"Grandfather, Josefina has a visitor staying with
her. This is María." Mariana speaks quietly, with her
eyes down, just as Josefina does when she talks to
her papá.

"Welcome, María," Esteban says.

"*Gracias.*" I clasp my hands against my skirt and
cast my eyes down to my moccasins.

Esteban doesn't say anything more, but one by one,
he offers each of us a little open-faced pie, filled with
fruit—some kind of berry.

"*Gracias,* Grandfather," Mariana says, and Josefina
and I echo her.

Esteban nods in a dignified way, but I think I spot
a small smile crinkling his cheeks.

The pies smell delicious, and I suddenly remember

how hungry I am. We sit on the ground near Esteban
and devour them.

"Do you think your grandfather will let you come
with us to see the horses for trade at the other side
of the *plaza*?" Josefina asks Mariana, as we wipe our
sticky fingers on Josefina's handkerchief.

Mariana doesn't reply but catches her grandfather's
eye. He nods and smiles, which must mean yes, because
Mariana takes one of my hands and Josefina takes the
other and they skip me off across the hard-packed dirt
to the side of the *plaza* nearest the huge church.

❋ *Turn to page 177.*

Light and music pour from the doorway of Señora Sanchez's house, greeting us. The large main room is transformed from the busy working scene of this morning.

Brightly dressed ladies and their partners are already twirling about to the music of a violin and two guitars played by three musicians in the corner. Older men and women are clustered on the *bancos* around the edges of the room, chatting and watching the dancing, while children play on the floor or sit in their laps. The twirling ladies seem as light as butterflies, their feet barely touching the floor. Francisca and Ana are immediately whirled away to dance. "Come on!" I tug at Josefina's hand. "Let's dance too."

Josefina looks shocked. "Oh no, María. We are too young to dance, of course. We can watch, though—here." She squeezes onto the corner of a *banco,* and I crowd in beside her.

Too young to dance? My hands pat in time to the music, and my body yearns to be out there twirling around. But I've been in Josefina's world long enough now to know that there are a lot of rules about how young girls behave.

At least there's still plenty to see. We take turns picking out the skirts we like best, and Josefina gives me a little background on the different couples. Francisca floats past with a handsome boy, glancing up at him through her eyelashes. Ana and her husband Tomás smile at each other as they dance. Then Josefina sits up a little straighter, and I follow her gaze. Tía Dolores and Señor Montoya are waltzing together. As if carried on the waves of music, they skim around the room.

"They dance so well together," I whisper to Josefina. Tía Dolores's face is lit with a warm smile as Señor Montoya inclines his dark head toward her.

"Yes, they do," Josefina murmurs back. She sounds a little surprised, as if the thought is new to her, and her eyes follow her aunt and her father as they dance in each other's arms.

The candles flicker and flare in their holders, throwing a magical glow over the room, and along one wall, I can see a cloth-covered table loaded with *tortillas,* stew, white cheese, bowls of custard, and *tamales.* The musicians are playing a lively tune, and the men stamp their heavy boots in time and the women clap their hands, their lovely shawls trailing

from their arms. Too soon, the musicians put down
their instruments for a break.

"Josefina, my dear, your hair is disheveled." Tía
Dolores has come up behind us. Josefina raises her
hand to her braid. "Here, come let me fix it."

She draws Josefina to a bench in a corner, and
I follow. Gently, she loosens the ribbon Josefina has
tied at the end of her braid, and with her fingers, she
untangles the wavy strands. "Your hair is getting
rough," she says softly. "When we're home, I'll give
you some lavender oil to comb into it. But you must
use it every night." Tía Dolores's face is soft as she
braids Josefina's hair again, and Josefina briefly rests
against her aunt's shoulder.

The swirl of the party seems to fade as I watch
the two of them together. All of a sudden, I wish that
my own mother were here—or that I were with her.
She used to braid my hair just like that, every morning
before school. And I would lean up against her, just
as Josefina leans against her aunt. I want to see my
own mother and let her braid my hair. With a pang,
I realize that I need to go home.

"Tía Dolores, Josefina, the party is wonderful, but

I—I think I need to go back to the house," I say.

"Do you mean you are tired, María?" Tía Dolores says. "I can ask Miguel to accompany you back home."

"*Sí, gracias,*" I say. I'm sure I can find a way to slip off quietly in the dark.

"No, María, don't go yet!" Josefina cries. "There's still the supper to eat."

"The party has stirred up some memories," I tell them. "I'm going to think—to try to remember my family. I'd like to find my way home to them. But I want to say *gracias* to both of you, for taking such good care of me."

Tía Dolores nods and smooths my hair back, just as she did to Josefina earlier. "We are glad you came to us, María," she says simply.

Josefina walks me to the door as Miguel waits just outside. "Good-bye, friend," I say. She hugs me tight, and I squeeze her back. *We're bonded through time,* I tell her silently, and I hope she can hear me in her heart.

❋ *Turn to page 171.*

servant serves tea and licorice-flavored *bizcochito* cookies, while Josefina's grandfather tells us a few adventures from his last trip with his caravan. I gather that he travels back and forth between Santa Fe and faraway Mexico City, buying trade goods in each place and selling them in the other. He keeps talking about *El Camino Real*, which must be the road between Mexico City and here.

Josefina recalls a time he brought her and her sisters a cone of the finest chocolate. "When Teresita made hot chocolate from it," she says, her eyes shining with the memory, "it was so creamy. And the taste when it spread across your tongue! Rich and sweet. I dreamed about it all that night."

It sounds odd that Josefina would be so enchanted just by *chocolate*, but even though she doesn't have as many things as I have, and even though she has to take a four-hour dusty wagon ride to Santa Fe, she doesn't seem unhappy. Not at all—actually, she seems *happy.*

Maybe the way you see your life matters more than the things you have. Josefina is just as happy in an adobe *house with no running water as I was in a city apartment,* I think, brushing a few *bizcochito* crumbs from my skirt.

"Abuelita, may I show María my favorite hill?"
Josefina asks, finishing her tea.

Josefina's grandmother smiles at us warmly. *"Sí,*
children, run along."

Quickly we clear away the teacups, and then I follow
Josefina out the front door. There is no dust out here,
just clear, sparkling air. Panting, with the wind blowing
our hair back, we climb a steep hill behind the house.
"Not too much farther," Josefina calls back, noticing that
I'm lagging. Her cheeks are pink, and little wisps of hair
have fallen from her braid into her face.

"I'm coming!" I call up to her. With a burst of speed,
I run to catch up, dirt and small rocks sliding beneath
my moccasins.

By the time I reach her, Josefina is standing at the
top of the hill with her hands on her hips, looking out.
"There! Isn't it beautiful?" she says. "This is my favorite
place in all of Santa Fe."

"Oooh," I breathe as I gaze out over the rooftops.
We can see all of Santa Fe from here—the low, flat
houses with narrow roads between, a silver slash of
river, and all around the city, big flat fields of ripe
crops. The mountains are dusted with dark green pine

trees and sprinkled with golden aspens. The snow
on the top seems almost close enough to touch. "It *is*
beautiful." And I mean it. It's a different kind of beauty
than the lights and soaring skyscrapers and bridges of
Chicago. It's quieter, closer to the earth. But for the first
time, I can see why Josefina loves this place. I think
I could grow to love it too.

I unbutton my waist pouch and draw out my flute.
Josefina is still looking out at the city, so I hold the
flute down by my side and stroke the soft clay with
my thumb. I was Birdy the musical girl once, but I lost
her somewhere between here and Chicago. I wonder
if maybe, just maybe, I could find her again.

"You know," I say slowly, "I think, from up here,
I can almost find my way home."

Josefina looks at me, surprised. "Truly, María?"

"Yes," I tell her. "I . . . think I just had to climb this
high first." *I can see it through time,* I tell her silently.
And it's time to go back.

❋ *Turn to page 175.*

I've barely played the last note of the mocking-bird's song before I find myself sprawled at the base of the rock, with a wet tongue licking my cheek. It's Daisy, and I'm back in my own world. Funny how the hills lit by the sunset look like home now.

I brush myself off and head into the warm, noisy house. My family is still gathered in the kitchen. Their faces look wonderfully familiar. I want to run over and hug them all, but since they think I've just been outside for a few minutes, I settle for pulling myself up to sit on the counter.

"Hey, sis," Henry says. He holds out the piece of paper I saw him showing Mom, right before I zoomed off to Josefina's world. "Check it out—a beginners' rock-climbing class. The outdoors club is putting it on. Do you want to take it with me?"

I study my brother's eager freckled face. Before Josefina, I would have said no right away. But now, exploring the desert doesn't sound so bad. "Yeah," I say slowly, examining the flyer. "That could be fun."

I look up and meet Dad's eyes. He raises his eyebrows as if to say, *Now that's a change.* I shrug.

Mom moves over to the stove and lifts the lid on the

steamer to check the *tamales.* A delicious spicy smell billows out. "Mmm," I inhale and slide down from the counter.

Dad wanders over casually. "Decided to give New Mexico a try, huh?" he murmurs out of the side of his mouth.

"I've been doing some thinking, is all," I tell him.

His forehead knits. "Must have been some serious thinking session."

I slide my fingers around my flute, safe in my pocket. "Oh, it was," I say. "You have no idea."

❀ *The End* ❀

To read this story another way and see how different choices lead to a different ending, turn back to page 108.

y feet can't resist the music. I grab Josefina's hands, and we whirl out into the shadows beside the house. From a window, a square of light and the sounds of music and pounding feet pour out. "One foot forward, step back, step forward," Josefina instructs. I stumble and almost fall on her, and we burst into laughter. I've missed having a friend to clown with, and I've missed being surrounded by music. I don't want to leave these things behind when I leave Josefina's world, I think.

And then the thought strikes me—maybe I don't have to.

Through the window, we hear everyone clap as the music ends with a flourish. Josefina and I look at each other and clap too, in our own little dancing space.

I look at my friend, who is breathlessly rearranging her *rebozo,* and I try to fix her warm face in my mind. I suddenly realize that being friends with Josefina hasn't made me forget Danielle, just like having Tía Dolores in her life hasn't made Josefina forget her mamá. I don't have to lose one friend just because I have another.

"Josefina, it's the oddest thing, but I think I know

how to find my way back to my home now," I tell my friend.

She lets her *rebozo* slide back down to her elbows. "Oh, María, have you remembered?"

I nod. "I've remembered . . . the important things."

"That's wonderful!" Josefina catches me by the arms and we swing around again, bathed in the warm light from the window, our feet carried on the wave of the music itself.

❋ *Turn to page 181.*

y stomach is fluttering the next morning when I push open the door to school, and it takes me a minute to realize that I'm nervous. *It's the first day of the rest of your life, it's the first day of the rest of your life, it's the first day of the rest of your life.* The old saying that my dad loves runs through my mind like the cars of a freight train going by on a track.

I can almost see Josefina walking beside me—it would be so much fun to show her my world now that I've seen hers! Still, she *is* with me. I've brought some of her strength and fun back with me through time, just like I've brought Chicago to Santa Fe with me in my heart.

I stop at the bulletin board that Audrey and I looked at yesterday. The Skit Club poster is still there. *Auditions on Tuesday!* it trumpets. As I examine it, I suddenly see myself covered in dust, jolting along in that wagon. I almost laugh. If I can embrace *that* experience, then I can handle this one, right? Josefina showed me that I'm a lot stronger than I think—and that Birdy is still inside me.

I turn on my heel and march down the hall. If I hurry, I can get to Mrs. McGlynn's classroom a few minutes before the bell. I have something important to ask Audrey—after all, auditions are next week and I know a great two-person scene we could perform.

Audrey is already at her desk when I hurry into the classroom.

"Hi," I say breathlessly.

She looks up from her book. "Hi." Her voice is neutral. She looks at me, waiting.

"I have this great book of scenes—all for two people." I pull it from my backpack. "Maybe...maybe we could practice one together. You know, for the Skit Club auditions." I hold my breath.

Audrey is still silent. Then she says, "Yeah. That would be fun." A smile spreads across her face. It's a warm smile that invites me in. Just like Josefina did.

❋ *The End* ❋

To read this story another way and see how different choices lead to a different ending, turn back to page 123.

orses offered for trade are tethered there, ranged out along the side of the *plaza,* all colors and sizes. I see a spotted black-and-white horse, a deep chestnut horse, a light tan one with a black mane and tail—that's called buckskin, I remember. There's even a frisky young palomino that's a beautiful blond color with a white-blond mane and tail.

Each horse wears a simple rope halter, tethered to a peg in the ground. The traders stand behind them in little knots, talking and waiting for offers. Here and there, men are walking up and down, studying the horses, looking in their mouths, and examining their shoulders and flanks.

"They're so beautiful!" I breathe, staring at their large, intelligent eyes and tossing heads. Their ears are pricked at all the noise and excitement of the *plaza,* and their nostrils flare, breathing in the unusual scents.

"Let's pick out horses for one another!" Josefina proposes. "I'll pick one for Mariana. María, you pick one for me, and Mariana will pick one for you. Then we'll ride our mounts back to our homes!"

We all laugh. "And we can race on the way!" I add. "Pick a fast one for me, Mariana."

"I like slow and steady," Josefina chimes in. "Sturdy too, María."

Mariana tilts her head at the adult horse-buyers and arranges her face into the same serious, brows-lowered expression they have. "Horse trading is serious business," she says in a pretend-deep voice.

Josefina bursts out laughing. "That's just what Papá always says."

"And my grandfather!" Mariana says in her own voice.

We walk up and down the row with our hands clasped behind our backs just like the adult horse-buyers. I look carefully at the big chestnut, who stands calmly with his noble head high, and at a fat, shaggy little pony with black spots like a Dalmatian. Beside him is a coal-black stallion who tosses his head and rolls his eye at me when I get too close. Josefina spends a long time looking at the palomino, and Mariana seems enchanted by a slender bay who snuffles at her hand.

After a few moments, I stop and face my friends. "All right!" I announce. "I've made my choice. How about you two?"

Josefina nods. "I have the perfect horse for Mariana," she says. She gestures toward a perky black mare beside us and makes a little bow toward Mariana. "My friend, I've chosen this fine black pony for you. Her eyes sparkle like yours, her mane is exactly the color of your hair, *and* she's not too tall, so you can mount by yourself."

Mariana grins. *"Gracias,* my friend. I accept my new horse!" We laugh.

Then it's my turn. I stand straight and pretend that I'm reading from a paper. I do a deep voice too, like an adult giving a speech. "My dearest Josefina," I begin. The girls giggle appreciatively. "For you, I have chosen a fine mount. He is bold and swift, yet he is young. He will require much instruction, and you are a skilled teacher." I give Josefina a significant look from under my brows, and she blushes a little and drops her eyes. "May I present—the palomino!" With a flourish, I extend my arm to the beautiful blond horse, who is little more than a colt.

"My beauty!" Josefina strokes the horse's velvety nose.

"María, I have a special horse for you," Mariana

says. "I didn't know which one I would pick until this moment. But now it's clear to me. Even though we just met, María, I hope you will be my friend, as you are Josefina's—so I'm choosing the chestnut horse for you." She nods toward a handsome animal who stands with his head raised, as if he's listening to us. "He's a beautiful brown—halfway between my black horse and Josefina's golden one. Do you see? Your horse joins the other two together. And we are three now, instead of two."

I feel a rush of affection for this girl who just met me, but who has accepted me as a friend. As I stand in the noisy, colorful *plaza,* I think of Audrey and how she wants to be my friend, even though we've just met. I don't want to leave Danielle behind—but maybe I don't have to. Josefina is still friends with Mariana, even though she welcomes me. Maybe being friends with Audrey doesn't mean that I have to lose Danielle.

I don't know. But I'm ready to try. I'm ready to ride the mockingbird's song back home.

❋ *Turn to page 182.*

ack in my own world that night, I curl up on my bed under my down comforter. It's *almost* as comfortable as Josefina's sheepskins. I reach for my phone on my bedside table and thumb through the online school directory. There she is. Audrey Capella. I take a deep breath and touch her number.

It's ringing. My stomach is fluttery.

"Hello?" she answers.

"Audrey, it's Birdy," I say. "You know, from school?"

She doesn't say anything. This is hard. But I think back to Josefina, reaching out to me when I was lost and alone. "I—I've been wondering. Do, um, do you want to come over one day after school? My brother, Henry, can pick us up. We could go for a hike."

She still doesn't say anthing, and my stomach sinks. I wish I'd never called.

"Sure," she says. "That would be fun."

A big grin splits my face. I feel like Josefina is watching me—and applauding.

❈ The End ❈

To read this story another way and see how different choices lead to a different ending, turn back to page 155.

he next day, back at school in my own time, I spot Audrey down at the end of the hallway. "Hi!" I call out, hurrying past the row of lockers. Audrey is stuffing a textbook into her backpack. She shuts her locker door and eyes me warily.

"Yeah?"

"I looked for you after English, but I must have missed you." I stop, breathing hard from my sprint down the hall.

She gazes at me steadily, but says nothing.

I swallow. This isn't going to be easy. But I summon up Josefina's face, and Mariana's, in front of me. They made friends with me when I really needed it. Now it's my turn. "Listen, I wasn't being very nice yesterday. I—I'm sorry. Moving here has been kind of hard, you know?"

She nods, just a little.

"I, um, I thought I wouldn't have anything in common with the people here at this school. But... I don't think that anymore," I tell her.

Audrey narrows her eyes. "How come?"

I think of skipping across the *plaza* with Josefina and Mariana, holding hands. "I had a few lessons.

From a very good teacher."

"Okay..." She looks a little confused.

"So...how about that ice-cream shop you were talking about yesterday? Do they have peach?" I grin at her and she grins back.

"They do! And it's so good."

Side by side, we push open the school doors and head out into the fresh New Mexico afternoon.

❈ *The End* ❈

To read this story another way and see how different choices lead to a different ending, turn back to page 26.

ABOUT Josefina's Time

New Mexico is part of the United States today, but in 1824 it belonged to Mexico, and before that it had belonged to Spain—just like California, Texas, and all the states in the Southwestern U.S. Almost everyone who lived in that region in Josefina's time was Spanish or Native American.

Most New Mexicans lived much the way Josefina and her family do, on *ranchos* or in small farming villages. Raising crops and animals in the high desert was not easy, so everyone, including children, worked hard and depended on one another. Children grew up with very close ties to their extended families and the few neighbors or villagers who lived nearby. The Catholic faith was an important part of people's everyday lives, and children usually had a special bond with their godparents, just as Josefina does with her godmother, Tía Magdalena.

When New Mexicans were sick or injured, they called on a *curandera* like Tía Magdalena for treatment. *Curanderas* knew how to make medicines from many kinds of plants. They were highly respected for their healing skills and their wisdom.

Children were expected to be respectful of grown-ups. To show respect, they kept their head and eyes down and their hands clasped in front of them, and didn't speak until they were spoken to. Still, children had lots of fun, too. Girls enjoyed string games, clapping games, and home-made dolls, and boys played a ball game called *shinny.* And everyone loved to share stories, songs, and riddles as they worked together or relaxed by the fire at night.

The Spanish settlers in New Mexico were allies and trading partners with their Pueblo Indian neighbors, but they were enemies of tribes such as the Navajo, Apache, and Comanche. Both sides raided each other fiercely and took women and children as captives, or *cautivas*. The Spanish used *cautivas* as servants; Indians often used them to do camp work or herd sheep. Torn from their families and their culture, *cautivas* must have suffered greatly. Some escaped and made their way back home, just as the Montoyas think Birdy did. However, most captives did not escape and eventually adjusted to their new lives, as Tía Dolores's servant Teresita did, but they probably never forgot the home they had left behind.

Santa Fe was the only town for hundreds of miles in any direction. As Birdy discovers, Santa Fe was not a big city, but it *was* a lively, exciting place where people from all around came to trade. The *Camino Real* was the wagon trail that connected Santa Fe with towns and cities far to the south. Trading caravans like Abuelito's traveled the *Camino Real* to bring necessities and luxuries from all around the world to Santa Fe, although the trip from Mexico City took months and crossed rugged, dangerous deserts and mountains. In 1821, a new wagon trail opened up between Santa Fe and Missouri. Known as the Santa Fe Trail, it began to draw American traders to New Mexico—the beginning of New Mexico's ties to the United States.

GLOSSARY of Spanish Words

Abuelita *(ah-bweh-LEE-tah)*—Grandma

Abuelito *(ah-bweh-LEE-toh)*—Grandpa

acequia *(ah-SEH-kee-ah)*—a ditch made to carry water to a farmer's fields

adiós *(ah-dee-OHS)*—good-bye

adobe *(ah-DOH-beh)*—a building material made of earth mixed with straw and water

banco *(BAHN-ko)*—a bench built into the wall of a room

bienvenida *(bee-en-veh-NEE-dah)*—welcome (used only to greet girls and women). The greeting for males and mixed groups is *bienvenido.*

bizcochito *(bees-ko-CHEE-toh)*—a kind of sugar cookie flavored with anise

buenos días *(BWEH-nohs DEE-ahs)*—good morning

cautiva *(kaw-TEE-vah)*—a female captive. (A male captive is a *cautivo.*)

chile *(CHEE-leh)*—a chili pepper

colcha *(KOHL-chah)*—a kind of embroidery made with long, flat stitches

curandera *(koo-rahn-DEH-rah)*—a woman who knows how to make medicines from plants and is skilled at healing

El Camino Real *(el kah-MEE-no rey-AHL)*—the main road or trail that ran from Mexico City to New Mexico. Its name means "Royal Road."

fandango *(fahn-DAHNG-go)*—a big celebration or party that includes a lively dance

gracias *(GRAH-see-ahs)*—thank you

La Jornada del Muerto *(lah hor-NAH-dah del MWEHR-toh)*—the name of an especially rugged, waterless part of El Camino Real. The words literally mean "The Route of the Dead Man."

Los Charcos del Perillo *(lohs CHAR-kohs del peh-REE-yo)*—the pools or springs of the little dog

mano *(MAH-no)*—a stone that is held in the hand and used to grind corn. Dried corn is put on a large flat stone called a *metate*, and then the mano is rubbed back and forth over the corn to break it down into flour.

masa *(MAH-sah)*—a dough made with cornmeal that is used in Mexican cooking

metate *(meh-TAH-teh)*—a large flat stone used with a *mano* to grind corn

patrón *(pah-TROHN)*—a man who has earned respect because he owns land and is a good leader of his family and his workers

piñón *(pee-NYOHN)*—a kind of short, scrubby pine that produces delicious nuts

plaza *(PLAH-sah)*—an open square in a village or town

pueblo *(PWEH-blo)*—a village of Pueblo Indians

rancho *(RAHN-cho)*—a ranch or farm where crops are grown and animals are raised

rebozo *(reh-BO-so)*—a long shawl worn by girls and women

ristra *(REE-strah)*—a string of fruit or vegetables that is hung up to dry, preserving the food for the winter

sala *(SAH-lah)*—a room in a house

Santa Fe *(SAHN-tah FEH)*—the capital city of New Mexico. Its name means "Holy Faith."

Señor *(seh-NYOR)*—Mr.

Señora *(seh-NYO-rah)*—Mrs.

sí *(SEE)*—yes

siesta *(see-ES-tah)*—a rest or nap in the afternoon

sombrita *(sohm-BREE-tah)*—little shadow, or an affectionate way to say "shadow." The Spanish word for "shadow" is *sombra.*

tamale *(tah-MAH-leh)*—spicy meat surrounded by cornmeal dough and cooked in a corn-husk wrapping

tía *(TEE-ah)*—aunt

tortilla *(tor-TEE-yah)*—a kind of flat, round bread made of corn or wheat

HOW TO SAY Spanish Names

Ana *(AH-nah)*

Andres *(ahn-DREHS)*

Carmen *(KAR-mehn)*

Clara *(KLAH-rah)*

Dolores *(doh-LO-rehs)*

Esteban *(EHS-teh-bahn)*

Felipe *(feh-LEE-peh)*

Francisca *(frahn-SEES-kah)*

García *(gar-SEE-ah)*

Jaramillo *(hah-rah-MEE-yo)*

Josefina *(ho-seh-FEE-nah)*

Luisa *(loo-EE-sah)*

Magdalena *(mahg-dah-LEH-nah)*

María *(mah-REE-ah)*

Mariana *(mah-ree-AH-nah)*

Mateo *(mah-TEH-o)*

Miguel *(mee-GEHL)*

Ofelia *(o-FEE-lyah)*

Sanchez *(SAHN-chehz)*

Teresita *(teh-reh-SEE-tah)*

Tomás *(toh-MAHS)*

Read more of JOSEFINA'S stories,

available from booksellers and at *americangirl.com*

❦ *Classics* ❧
Josefina's classic series, now in two volumes:

Volume 1:
Sunlight and Shadows
Josefina and her sisters are
excited when Tía Dolores
comes to their *rancho*, bringing
new ideas, new fashions, and
new challenges. Can Josefina
open her heart to change
and still hold on to precious
memories of Mamá?

Volume 2:
Second Chances
Josefina makes a wonderful
discovery: She has a gift for
healing. Can she find the
courage and creativity to mend
her family's broken trust in an
americano trader and keep her
family whole and happy when
Tía Dolores plans to leave?

❦ *Journey in Time* ❧
Travel back in time—and spend a day with Josefina!

Song of the Mockingbird
Spend a cozy evening at the *rancho*, come face-to-face with a
snarling mountain lion, or visit the lively market in Santa Fe.
Choose your own path through this multiple-ending story!

❦ *Mystery* ❧
Another thrilling adventure with Josefina!

Secrets in the Hills
Josefina has heard tales of treasure buried in the hills, and of
a ghostly Weeping Woman who roams at night. But she never
imagined the stories might be true—until a mysterious stranger
arrives at her *rancho*.

Sunlight and Shadows

A Josefina Classic

Volume 1

What happens to Josefina?
Find out in the first volume of her classic stories.

osefina had gathered a basketful of onions when suddenly she stood up. Francisca stood up, too, and the girls looked at each other.

"Is it . . . ?" Francisca began.

"Shhh . . ." said Josefina, holding her finger to her lips. She tilted her head and listened hard. Yes! There it was. She could hear the rumble and squeak of wooden wheels that meant only one thing. The caravan was coming!

Francisca heard, too. The girls smiled at each other, grabbed their baskets, and ran as fast as they could back through the gate. "The caravan! It's coming!" they shouted. "Ana! Clara! It's coming!" They dropped their baskets outside the kitchen door as Clara rushed out to join them.

The three girls dashed across the front courtyard and flew up the steps of the tower in the south wall. The window in the tower was narrow, so Josefina knelt and looked out the lower part. Francisca and Clara stood behind her and looked over her head.

At first, all they saw was a cloud of dust stirring on the road from the village. Then the sound of the wheels grew louder and louder. Soon they heard the jingle of harnesses, dogs barking, people shouting, and the village church bell ringing. Next they saw soldiers coming over the hill with the sun glinting on their buttons and guns. Then came mule after mule. It looked like a hundred or more to Josefina. The mules were carrying heavy packs strapped to their backs. She counted thirty carts pulled by plodding oxen. The carts lumbered along on their two big wooden wheels. There were four-wheeled wagons as well. And so many people! Too many to count! There were cart drivers, traders, and whole families of travelers. There were herders driving sheep, goats, and cattle. People from town and Indians from the nearby pueblo village walked along with the caravan to welcome it.

Francisca stood on tiptoe to see better. She put her hands on Josefina's shoulders. "Don't you love to think about all the places the caravan has been?" she asked. "And all the places the things it brings come from, too?"

"Yes," said Josefina. "They come from all over the world, up the Camino Real, right to *our* door!"

Most of the caravan stopped and set up camp midway between the town and the rancho. But many

of the cart drivers camped closer to the house, in a shady area next to the stream. Josefina saw Papá ride his horse up to one of the big, four-wheeled wagons. He waved to its driver.

"That's Abuelito!" Josefina cried. She pointed to the driver of the four-wheeled wagon. "Look! Papá is greeting him. See? There he is!"

Francisca leaned forward. "Who's that tall woman sitting next to Abuelito?" she wondered aloud. "She's greeting Papá as if she knows him."

But Josefina and Clara had already turned away from the window. They hurried down from the tower. Josefina ran to the kitchen and stuck her head in the door. "Come on," she said to Ana. "Papá and Abuelito are on their way up to the house."

"Oh dear, oh dear," fussed Ana as she wiped her hands and smoothed her hair. "There's still so much to do. I'll never be ready for the fandango."

When Papá led Abuelito's big wagon up to the front gate, Josefina was the first to run out and greet it. Francisca, Clara, and Ana were close behind. Josefina thought she'd never seen a sight as wonderful as Abuelito's happy face. He handed the reins to the

woman next to him and climbed down.

"My beautiful granddaughters!" said Abuelito. He
kissed them as he named them. "Ana, and Francisca!
Clara, and my little Josefina! Oh, God bless you! God
bless you! It is good to see you! This was the finest trip
I've ever made! Oh, the adventures, the adventures!
But I am getting too old for these trips. They make me
old before my time. This is my last trip. My last."

"Oh, Abuelito!" said Francisca, taking his arm and
laughing. "You say that every time!"

Abuelito threw back his head and laughed, too.
"Ah, but this time I mean it," he said. "I've brought
a surprise for you." He turned and held out his hand
to the tall woman on the wagon. "Here she is, your
Tía Dolores. She has come back to live with her mamá
and me in Santa Fe. Now I have no reason to go to
Mexico City ever again!"

Josefina and her sisters looked so surprised, Papá
and Abuelito laughed at them. Tía Dolores took
Abuelito's hand and gracefully swung herself down
from the wagon seat.

Papá smiled at her. "You see, Dolores? You have
surprised my daughters as much as you surprised me,"

he said. "Welcome to our home."

"Gracias," Tía Dolores answered. She smiled at Papá and then she turned to the sisters. "I've looked forward to this moment for a long time!" she said to them. "I've wanted to see all of you! My dear sister's children!"

She spoke to each one in turn. "You're very like your mamá, Ana," she said. "And Francisca, you've grown so tall and so beautiful! Dear Clara, you were barely three years old when I left. Do you remember?"

Tía Dolores took Josefina's hand in both of her own. She bent forward so that she could look closely at Josefina's face. "At last I meet you, Josefina," she said. "You weren't even born when I left. And look! Here you are! Already a lovely young girl!" Tía Dolores straightened again. Her eyes were bright as she looked at all the sisters. "I'm so happy to see you all. It's good to be back."

The girls were still too surprised to say much, but they smiled shyly at Tía Dolores. Ana was the first to collect herself. "Please, Abuelito and Tía Dolores. Come inside and have a cool drink. I'm sure you're tired and thirsty." She led Tía Dolores inside the gate. "You must excuse us, Tía Dolores," she said. "We haven't prepared any place for you to sleep."

"Goodness, Ana!" said Tía Dolores. "You didn't know I was coming. I didn't know myself, really, until the last minute. I've been caring for my dear aunt in Mexico City all these years. Bless her soul! She died this past spring. It was just before Abuelito's caravan arrived. I had no reason to stay. So, I joined the caravan to come home."

"Yes," Abuelito said to the girls. "Your grandmother will be so pleased! Wait till Dolores and I get to Santa Fe the day after tomorrow! What a surprise, eh?"

Josefina could not take her eyes off Tía Dolores as everyone sat down together in the family sala. The room's thick walls and small windows kept it cool even in the heat of the afternoon.

Francisca whispered, "Isn't Tía Dolores's dress beautiful? Her sleeves must be the latest style from Europe."

But Josefina hadn't noticed Tía Dolores's sleeves, or anything else about her clothes. *This is Tía Dolores,* she kept thinking. *This is Mamá's sister.*

Josefina studied Tía Dolores to see if she looked

like Mamá. Mamá had been the older of the two sisters, but Tía Dolores was much taller. She didn't have Mamá's soft, rounded beauty, Josefina decided, nor her pale skin or dark, smooth hair. Everything about Tía Dolores was sharper somehow. Her hands were bigger. Her face was more narrow. She had gray eyes and dark red hair that was springy. Her voice didn't sound like Mamá's, either. Mamá's voice was high and breathy, like notes from a flute. Tía Dolores's voice had a graceful sound. It was as low and clear as notes from a harp string. But when Tía Dolores laughed, Josefina was startled. Her laugh sounded so much like Mamá's! If Josefina closed her eyes, it might be Mamá laughing.

There was a great deal of laughter in the family sala that afternoon as Abuelito told the story of his trip. Josefina sat next to Abuelito, her arms wrapped around her knees. She was happy.

About the Author

First, EMMA CARLSON BERNE thought she was going to be a college professor, so she went to graduate school at Miami University in Ohio. After that, she taught horseback riding in Boston and Charleston, South Carolina. *Then* Emma found out how much she enjoys writing for children and young adults. Since that time, she has authored more than two dozen books and often writes about historical figures such as Sacagawea, Helen Keller, Christopher Columbus, and the artist Frida Kahlo. Emma lives in a hundred-year-old house in Cincinnati, Ohio, with her two little boys and her husband.